THE COWBOY'S REALITY BRIDE

LORANA HOOPES

Copyright © 2019 by Lorana Hoopes

All rights reserved.

No part of this book may be reproduced in any form or by any electronic or mechanical means, including information storage and retrieval systems, without written permission from the author, except for the use of brief quotations in a book review.

❦ Created with Vellum

NOTE FROM THE AUTHOR

I have been so blessed to meet amazing authors in my journey, and I am excited to be joining with a few of them to bring you The Blushing Brides Series.

This book is dedicated to the amazing cast of Mary Poppins that I worked with this year. A majority of this book was written backstage. Dallas, Cassidy, and Kanina were all great friends who allowed me to use them in my novel. I'd also like to thank my high school friends: Maryanne, Jennifer, Tracey, Meredith, and Steven. It wouldn't have been the same without you.

As you can tell, there's a bit of me in this book. There's even more in the free bonus I'm offering. Be sure to read to the end to find out how you can pick up that free bonus.

I hope you love this story of Tyler and Laney. If you do, please leave a review at your retailer. It really does make a difference because it lets people make an informed decision about books.

Sign up for Lorana Hoopes's newsletter and get her book, Once Upon a Star, as a welcome gift. Get Started Now!

The other books in the Blushing Bride series:
　The Reality Bride's Baby

The Producer's Unlikely Bride

The Cop's Fiery Bride

The Soldier's Stalwart Bride

1

*L*aney Swann clutched the strap of her black Tory Burch bag tighter as she weaved in and out of the crowded sidewalk. Why did the crowd have to be so thick today, on the one day she overslept? Normally, she was out the door by six am giving her plenty of time to travel uptown, stop at the bustling coffee shop, and walk into work by eight. However, sleep had eluded her last night, and she'd slept through her alarm waking instead to the soft rays of the sun peeking in her window. Now, she was paying the price.

    She flipped her delicate silver watch around to read the face and quickened her pace. She was going to be so late, and Victoria Bonavich detested tardiness. It was a fireable offense in her book if you stepped in the office even a minute late, and Laney couldn't afford to lose this job. The call offering her this job and a move to New York had been a dream come true. She'd moved away from home with big dreams but a small savings after college. If she lost this job, there would be no paying her rent, and she'd have to go home. A nervous spring coiled in her stomach. She couldn't lose this job.

"Watch it!" The man's gruff tone only spurred her on as she squeezed between him and another man with a cell phone glued to his ear. Both wore immaculate suits and tight expressions under their furrowed brows.

"Sorry," she called back over her shoulder as she lengthened her stride. It was rude not to turn fully around when she offered her apology, and Laney's mother would have her head if she ever knew but turning around would cost precious seconds and she had none to spare. Her heart thudded a constant drum of the precious seconds slipping away. How many did she have left?

A tendril of blond hair appeared in her vision and she blew it off her forehead with an exasperated breath. Great. Now, not only was she late, but her hair was eking out of its sprayed mold, another issue she would have to remedy before seeing Madame Bonavich or The Man-eater as they called her in the office. Unkempt hair was only slightly better than tardiness in Madame Bonavich's eyes.

The woman was fearsome. With short grey hair, hawkish eyes, and thin lips that rarely smiled, she exuded a no-nonsense air wherever she went and reminded Laney of a fierce predator in constant search of prey. But Laney enjoyed working for her. Mostly. She had learned much in the six months she had been at the agency even though she was still just an unknown assistant to Madame Bonavich.

Actually, she had learned everything from Myra, the makeup artist she assisted before photo shoots, but Laney still hoped to become Madame Bonavich's assistant one day. Then she would have a chance at becoming a well-known makeup artist herself. At least she had received the promotion to coffee gopher the last month. It gave her a chance to interact with The Man-eater if only for a minute.

However, today, it could be her downfall. Only fifteen minutes remained to obtain the coffee and return to the office, and it wasn't looking good. Time was slipping away faster than her feet were carrying her. Laney stepped up her pace a little more. Not too fast though. The last thing she wanted to do was trip, and sadly, she was a bit of a klutz.

"Excuse me," she said as she pushed through another clump of pedestrians. Why did it seem as if people walked slower and in impenetrable groups whenever she was in a hurry? The busy city was always like this, she knew that, but her need to move at a faster pace exaggerated the normal bustling bog and edged her anxiety up another notch. An eye twitch joined the nervous stomach.

At last the coffee shop came into view. Sweet relief flowed over her even though her feet ached already from the rigorous pace she had set the moment she stepped out of her door. The four-inch heels were a requirement in the agency - something that had taken Laney months to get used to - and though she agreed they added style to her outfit, her feet were not fans. They screamed for a nightly soak, and she had purchased so much Epsom Salt in the last few months she should buy stock in the company.

A sigh billowed out of her lips as she pulled open the door, and the spring coiled tighter. At least four other people stood in line. Laney bit her lip and checked her watch again. Thirteen minutes remained. Her foot began a rhythmic cadence on the floor, the impatient tapping garnering a few irritated stares, but Laney didn't care. She didn't have time to care.

The man in front of her turned around. "You appear to be in an awful hurry. Would you like to take my spot?"

"Could I? That would be amazing." Laney stepped in front of the man but remained facing him. He had the most amazing eyes. Blue with tiny green flecks. She was a sucker for eyes. Window to the soul and all that. "My boss is a bit of a time manager, if you know what I mean. If I don't get her coffee and get back to her in just over ten minutes," she blew out a puff of air as she shook her head side to side, "I don't even know what will happen, but it won't be good."

The man said nothing, just raised an eyebrow at her, but Laney couldn't shut her mouth. Perhaps it was his beautiful blue eyes - blue eyes were her kryptonite.

"Normally, it's not an issue, but last night sleep evaded me. I just tossed and turned - my sheets look like a tornado touched down on them." She made a swirling motion with her finger. "So, when my alarm clock rang, I guess I didn't hear it. Though I must have turned it off because it wasn't still beeping when I did finally wake up. I woke up to the sun if you can believe that. I never get to wake up to the sun, but of course it made me late. And now I'm in danger of incurring her wrath." Laney paused her verbal spew as the man's lips pulled into a smirk. "What?"

He pointed a finger toward the register behind her. "I believe it's your turn to order."

"Oh, right, thank you." A heated flush crawled up her face as she turned to face the woman behind the counter. She had made a fool of herself with the handsome man behind her. Why did her mouth always seem to run unchecked whenever she was nervous?

"Can I help you?" The woman's voice was flat, but perhaps that was simply her personality because her facial features held no emotion either. Not even a hint of a smile pulled at the lips under her bored brown eyes.

"Yes, I uh..." Laney cleared her throat and forced her mind to focus. She could berate herself later. "I need a tall caramel macchiato and-" she shook her head. Even after a month, she didn't have Madame Bonavich's order memorized, but who could blame her? It had to be the longest order she had ever seen. "Sorry, just a second." Her fingers rifled in her purse until they touched a folded piece of paper. She pulled it out and unfolded it. "A double ristretto venti half soy nonfat organic chocolate brownie iced vanilla double shot gingerbread Frappuccino extra hot with foam upside down double blended, one Sweet N Low and one NutraSweet."

The cashier blinked, and a momentary shell-shocked expression covered her impassive face. Then composure set in, and she rang up the order and picked up two cups. Laney felt sorry for the woman. Her job required her to read off an order, but this woman had to put that nonsense on a cup in a way that the barista making the coffee would understand. Not for the first time, Laney wondered if Madame Bonavich ordered this drink because she enjoyed it or because she relished putting others through the ringer.

With the bill paid, Laney continued down the line to stand at the other end where the barista placed completed drinks. She kept her gaze low to avoid her eyes seeking the nice man again. He didn't need any more verbal diarrhea from her.

Nine more minutes. She was cutting it so close. The office sat just around the corner, but her high heels kept her from running, so she'd have to opt for long strides and hope for the best.

"Caramel Macchiato and gingerbread frap," the barista called as she placed the two drinks down.

"Thank you." Laney flashed the woman an apologetic smile as she grabbed the drinks.

As she pushed open the door, she realized she should have asked for a tray. A cup in each hand made it nearly impossible to adjust her purse strap which kept threatening to slip off her shoulder with every step. Unable to stop, Laney adjusted her body by throwing her right shoulder as high into the air as possible in hopes gravity would keep the purse strap there.

She must look a sight, hunched over to one side like a modern-day Quasimodo. Madame Bonavich would blow her lid if she saw Laney, but it was this or arrive late with the woman's coffee, and Laney honestly didn't know which would be worse.

A sigh of relief spilled from her mouth as the office came into view. She would not chance looking at her watch, but she figured she had a few minutes to spare. However, she also had a conundrum. How was she going to open the door? She hated taking the chance but stacking one cup on top of the other appeared to be the quickest option.

Before her mind changed, she set the venti on top of her Grande and secured it with her chin. Then she reached for the door handle, but as her fingertips brushed the cold metal, the door swung open.

The force knocked her backwards. Her chin lifted from the lid of the cup, and without something to secure it, it teetered. Laney observed in slow-motion horror as the cup tipped off its perch and onto her chest. The lid popped off and flew through the air as the contents of the drink spilled down Laney's front.

Her body unfroze when the searing hot liquid broached her skin. Laney jumped farther back sending the venti cup crashing to the pavement - the liquid spilling out like caramel colored blood.

"I'm so sorry. Can I help?"

Anger flared in her stomach, and Laney flicked her eyes up to take in the perpetrator before she let loose her vitriol on him. However, the flame fizzled at the sight of the young man with glasses who stood gaping at her. His wide eyes held an apology and his baby face placed his age in his early twenties - probably a college intern. She swallowed the harsh words she wanted to bark at him. If she'd had Madame Bonavich's coffee order written anywhere else, she would give him the paper and tell him to go replace the coffee. It would be late, but perhaps late was better than never, but she didn't.

"No, it's fine. I'll take care of it." She didn't know how exactly. The only option she had was giving Madame Bonavich her drink which probably wouldn't sit well with the woman. She could only hope her boss was in a good mood and that was like hoping for it to be Christmas every day.

"Again, I'm so sorry." The man ducked his head and scurried away looking very much like a scolded puppy with its tail between its legs.

Laney spared one glance at her formerly white shirt now stained brown and sighed. She was late; she didn't have the woman's coffee; and she looked like a slob. These were not the makings of a good day.

2

Tyler Hall stared at the woman across the table from him as if she were a stranger and not the woman he'd been dating for the last six months. "I'm sorry, what did you say?"

She let out an exasperated sigh and flicked her chestnut hair over her shoulder. "I'm leaving, Tyler. I thought I could handle this, that it might be fun, but there is nothing to do in this town, and I'm bored. You work all day and you don't even drink-"

Heat erupted in Tyler and he interrupted her, "I told you why I don't drink."

Sierra rolled her eyes. "I know, you don't drink because you're a recovering alcoholic, but I'm not. Tyler, I'm twenty-six years old, and I want to have a little fun."

"I'm fun." Tyler couldn't believe this was happening again. It was becoming an alarming precedent. "I have fun."

"Hanging out with your friend Aaron and his wife is not my idea of fun. I mean it's fine for them to stay home and play scrabble - they're married - but I want to do more. I want to go out and not worry if I have a drink." She lifted her glass of wine as if in punctuation and took a sip.

Or a few drinks, Tyler thought to himself. He should have known when he met Sierra at the town social. She'd been tipsy that night but had assured him it was only because it was her friend's birthday. They'd avoided drinks after that, but lately Sierra had insisted they go out to eat instead of eating at his ranch, and she'd ordered a drink every time. "I've never stopped you from drinking."

"No, you haven't, but it hasn't made me feel any less guilty, and I don't want to feel guilty." She reached across the table and took ahold of his hand. "We're just not right for each other, Tyler. Surely you know that."

His gaze fell to their hands. Yes, he knew that. He'd noticed her distancing herself in the last month, and it wasn't like this was new to him. His last three relationships had ended similarly. Still, past experiences never seemed to prepare him when the words left their mouths. He eased his hand out of her grip and leaned back. "You're right, Sierra. We aren't right for each other." He reached into his pocket and pulled out his wallet. A twenty should be enough to cover his meal. She could pay for her own. He dropped the twenty on the table and pushed back his chair. "I wish you the best."

Her eyes widened, and her demeanor shifted. "You

don't have to leave right now, Tyler. At least eat." She glanced around the crowded restaurant but kept her voice low.

"I'm no longer hungry, Sierra, but that should cover my order."

"Tyler." Her voice held an angry hiss, but she still didn't raise her volume. Probably she hoped he would come back and not make a scene. He wondered briefly if she even had money to pay for her order but found he didn't care. He was tired of doing what everyone else wanted.

The cool air matched his mood as he stepped out of the restaurant and walked toward his truck. Lights from a nearby bar called to him, but he looked away. Aaron. He needed to see Aaron. That would calm him down and keep him from drinking. He'd been sober long before Sierra, and he was determined to remain that way after her.

"So, what happened?" Aaron asked as he flipped over the ribs he'd been cooking when Tyler arrived.

Tyler pulled his coat tighter and leaned closer to the warmth emanating from the grill. "Sierra and I broke up. Or she broke up with me, rather."

"Man, I'm sorry. You've had rough luck with women lately." Aaron closed the grill lid to give the meat a little more heat.

Tyler scoffed. "Yeah, rough doesn't really begin to describe it." His last three girlfriends had all said similar things. They loved him, but they needed excitement or someone with more drive. Tyler had drive, but his drive was focused on his ranch - keeping it afloat and obtaining more cattle. They just didn't understand his drive, and part of that was because two of the last three had been city girls thinking they wanted a change but realizing later the country was not the change they sought. Dierdre had been a country girl, but it turned out she wanted to try the other side as well. She'd left him for a lawyer in a big city. At least he hoped that's what it had been because otherwise it was him, and he didn't know how to fix that.

"Maybe you should go on that reality show that Nancy watches. Marry a Cowboy or something like that."

A deep chuckle issued from Tyler's throat. "Yeah, that's what I need - the whole world knowing I can't keep a girl around. That doesn't sound like something that would draw in the type of woman I'm looking for."

"No, I'm serious. Don't tell anyone, but Nancy made me watch an episode with her. I think it was the first one. They brought in like thirty beautiful women for this guy to choose from."

"A beautiful outside isn't everything." Tyler hated it when people only focused on outer appearances. Yes, it was necessary to feel attracted to the other person, but beauty faded. Personality was more important to Tyler as it would be around long after the looks went away.

"But it never hurts. Anyway, they pay for the dates and you get to know the women. Maybe it's worth a try. Widen the pool as it were."

"Can you imagine me on television?" The thought sent Tyler laughing and Aaron quickly joined in.

The sliding glass door opened, and Nancy stepped out. A simple woman, she usually opted for flannel shirts and jeans. Today, a blanket shawl sat on her shoulders as well. "What's so funny?" She looked from one man to the other.

"Aaron thinks I should try to be a contestant on some reality dating show," Tyler said as his laugh faded.

Nancy's eyes widened to the size of half dollars. "Who Wants to Marry a Cowboy?"

"Yeah, that's the one," Aaron said as his own laughter fizzled. "Sierra broke up with him."

Nancy's smile faded, and her forehead wrinkled in a sympathetic expression. Her hand landed on Tyler's shoulder. "Oh, Tyler, I'm so sorry to hear that, but I think you would be great on the show. From what I understand you fill out a survey and they find women that match what you like. It might be a great opportunity to meet women you wouldn't normally."

Tyler chuffed as he looked from Aaron to Nancy. He'd known Aaron since high school and Nancy since just after graduation. There was a time they were clearly separate people but after being married for a decade, it was harder to tell where Nancy ended, and Aaron began. "You two sound so alike." Tyler shook his head. Would he ever find a love like Nancy and Aaron had?

"I'm serious. In fact, I'm going to go look up the requirements right now. I'm sure it's easy." Before either man could say a word, Nancy spun and disappeared into the house, her brown ponytail flying out behind her.

"Why do I have the feeling that I'm going to be

auditioning whether I like it or not?" Tyler asked as he leaned back against the porch railing.

"Because you know my wife." Aaron grinned and opened the grill to check the meat.

That Tyler did. Nancy was a determined woman and she almost always accomplished whatever she set out to do.

3

*L*aney paused outside the ornate office door gathering her courage. With no idea how the next few minutes would go, she could only hope for the best. She took a final deep breath, squared her shoulders, and pushed open the door. Victoria Bonavich stood in front of the large glass window as Laney entered the room.

"You're late." Her cold voice sent a chill down Laney's spine.

"I know, ma'am, and I'm so sorry. There was a snafu-"

"I have no time for your snafus." The woman cut her off with a flick of her wrist. "Do you have my coffee?"

Laney grimaced as she held out the drink. "Well, that's what I was trying-"

"We don't try here. We do, or we get fired." She swiped the cup from Laney's outstretched hand and before Laney said another word, she tilted it back, but her face changed as the coffee hit her tongue and instead of swallowing it, she spat it out across the floor. "What is this disgusting concoction? This is not my drink."

Laney's eyes dropped to the floor and her hands folded together. "No, it isn't, but that's what I was trying to tell you. An intern bumped into me at the front door and your coffee spilled. I didn't have time to go and get another one, so I gave you mine. If you'd like, I can go now-"

The woman's icy eyes regarded Laney sending a chill all the way down to her toes. "What I'd like is for you to go and pack your things."

No, this couldn't be happening. Dread flooded Laney, and though she knew she shouldn't, she opened her mouth, "But Madame Bonavich, it was my first mistake-"

"I don't have time for mistakes or incompetence. You have proven you are prone to both."

"But, I need this job."

"And I need competent people. We're done now." As if to punctuate her statement, Victoria Bonavich walked over to the trash can, held the cup over it with her manicured claws, glanced back at Laney for dramatic effect, and dropped the full cup of coffee into it.

Anger burned through Laney, and she bit her lip to keep from saying anything more. Madame Bonavich not only ruled her company but half of New York. Laney might have lost her job here, but if she pushed the issue, she would never get hired at any other modeling agency in New York.

"Yes ma'am." Laney nodded and backed out of the room. Tears burned at the back of her eyes, and she blinked them back. She was not going to let them fall. At least not until she was out of this cursed office.

When she reached her desk, she pulled out the small cardboard box that lived under the right bottom drawer. Every desk came with one as employees didn't last long with Madame Bonavich. Either they quit, or she fired them within a few months' time. Laney had lasted longer than most.

"Oh no." Sofie, the other errand girl, regarded her with sympathetic eyes. "What happened?"

Laney shrugged and swallowed the lump building in her throat. "I was late and didn't have her coffee. Course it wasn't my fault, but that didn't matter to her. Hope you don't end up with the job now."

Laney took the few items off her desk and placed them in the box. There weren't many. The agency only allowed five personal items. Laney had fewer. A photograph of her parents, one of her and her best friends in high school, and one of Dallas Nixon. He had been her crush in high school though he hadn't known she was alive. Laney kept it as a reminder to never be invisible again. That was part of why she had taken this job in the first place.

She packed them in the nondescript box wondering with each one what she would do now. Her rent was atrocious, and her paycheck barely covered it each month. She had none in savings, and who knew how long it would take her to find another job.

"Please tell Myra thank you for all her tips when you see her and best of luck to you," Laney said to Sofie as she tucked the box under her arm and headed for the door. Sofie's response was a wide-eyed look full of fear.

Though the crowd had thinned a little, Laney no longer felt the rush as she began the long walk home. People pushed by her, but she hardly noticed as her mind ran through all her possible options. There weren't many. She knew almost no one in the city even though she had been here for six months. Unlike the city in Texas she grew up in, the people here were less than friendly and kept to themselves more often than not.

"Lord, I could use some guidance here," she whispered as she entered her apartment. The words felt foreign in her mouth. Laney hadn't prayed in a while, and a part of her wondered if losing her job had been God's way of reaching out to her. She'd been too busy to attend church and Sundays seemed to be Madame Bonavich's favorite day to require errands.

As she shut the door behind her, she noticed the blinking light of the answering machine. Almost no one used them anymore preferring cell phones and voicemail instead, but her mother was inept with technology and had insisted on sending her with the answering machine when she moved. Laney had to look twice because the machine rarely blinked. Few people outside of her work called her and they all had her cell phone number.

She pressed the play button and her mother's voice filled the room. "Is it time to speak now? I hope I'm talking at the right time. Laney, it's your mother. I got a call from an old friend of yours from high school. Maryanne

Nguyen. I guess she didn't have your new number, but she wants to connect with you. I wasn't sure if I should give out your number, but she left hers. It's... now where did I put that paper? Oh, here it is. It's 555-923-7555. Wow, that is a lot of fives. Okay, well I hope this gets to you. I think I just have to hang up, right?"

Laney chuckled at her mother's message and shook her head. Even in real life, her mother was often as scatterbrained as she sounded on the machine. Lane reached for the delete button, but curiosity stopped her. What had Maryanne wanted? Laney hadn't been popular in high school, but she'd had a group of friends, brainy misfits like herself who didn't fit in anywhere else and who were united by one teacher and a competitive drama league. Nearly every weekend for four years, they had traveled to tournaments where they competed in acting, debating, and speech competitions. Somewhere Laney still had a ton of trophies she had won. At one time, she had even considered pursuing teaching if she could coach kids like herself, but then she'd felt the need to be something more. To be noticed.

The group had promised to keep in touch after high school, but as they had all gone to separate colleges, staying in touch proved challenging and sometime in her sophomore year, Laney had lost contact with them.

She played the message one more time to make sure she had the number right. Then she pulled out her cell phone and punched it in. It rang only once before a breathless voice answered. "Hello?"

"Hi, is this Maryanne?" Laney didn't recognize the voice on the other end, but it had been nearly a decade since she'd spoken with her friend.

"Yes, who is this?" She'd taken a deep breath and her voice was all business now.

"It's Laney. Laney Swann. My mother said you called looking for me."

"Laney? Is it really you? Oh, thank goodness, I was so afraid you wouldn't get my message." Even though it had been years, *this voice* Laney recognized. Maryanne had been the quiet Korean girl, but when you got her excited, she was like an adrenaline filled wind up doll. Her voice ramped up, and she could speak ninety to nothing. "Are you still a makeup artist? I thought that's what you were studying after high school and I didn't make it back for the ten-year reunion - not sure if you did - but I asked around. Well, with the people I'm still in touch with. Mainly through social media. I'm not sure I have anyone's phone number anymore. I certainly don't have any memorized anymore, so unless they're in my phone, they cease to exist."

Laney chuckled trying to replay the conversation to see if there had been a question in there.

"So, are you?" Maryanne repeated.

"Am I what?"

"Still a makeup artist."

"Oh, um." How did she answer this? She'd studied makeup and design in college. She'd worked a few jobs after college. Laney considered herself a makeup artist, but she'd done nothing but hold supplies for a makeup artist for the last six months. "Well, I'm kind of between jobs right now, but-"

Maryanne squealed on the other end. "Oh my gosh. This is perfect timing. I need you. Well, not me, but the company I work for. See, I work for NGN studios and we do a reality TV show, and our normal makeup artist decided to take maternity leave early. We're about to film a new season, and we need a makeup artist. I told them I knew someone and that I'd call you and see if you could do it. So, can you?"

"Can I what?" Laney's head was spinning. She'd forgotten just how fast Maryanne could speak.

"Can you come to California and be our makeup artist? It will be super easy, and we'll cover the costs to fly you out here and set you up."

"Set me up?"

"Yeah, lodging. The show takes four to six weeks to film usually. Oh my gosh, this will be so much fun. Like our own mini reunion."

Four to six weeks? Laney couldn't be gone four to six weeks. How would she pay her rent? She couldn't possibly leave her life in New York, but as she looked around her tiny apartment, she wondered if that were true. Her kitchen was smaller than her bathroom had been growing up. The living room doubled as her bedroom with a fold out bed, and none of the walls were decorated. Laney wasn't sure if that was from lack of effort or lack of time, but what she did know was that her apartment was depressing.

So, what if she moved? She could pack up her things and put them in storage near her mother which would be cheaper than renting an apartment. Her lease was up for renewal at the end of the month anyway. She could just not renew, take this job, and start over. Laney wasn't exactly sure how or what she would do when she started over, but this plan would buy her a little time to figure it out anyway.

"Okay, I'll do it. Do I have time to stop and see my mom first? I haven't been home in ages and I need to ask a favor of her."

"Sure, I'll purchase your ticket and send you the details. Oh my gosh, this is going to be so much fun."

4

Tyler leaned back in his chair stuffed from the dinner. If he ate anymore, he would have to undo the button on his jeans, but he typically only ate this well when he was with Tyler and Nancy, so he always let himself splurge a little. "Those ribs were amazing, Aaron."

"And how about my coleslaw?" Nancy's lips turned out in a pout as if hurt by his words, but Tyler knew she was pulling his leg.

"Also amazing. My apologies. I didn't mean to offend the chef."

A coy smile spread across her lips and a twinkle sparked in her eyes. "Well, there's a way you can make it up to me."

Tyler's stomach filled with lead. The reality show. He could tell from the gleam in her eye she wanted him to audition for the reality show. "Nancy, I-"

"Hear me out," she blurted as she leaned forward. "It's

an easy application. We have to send in a short video of you and then you have to fill out the profile. If you're worried, you probably won't even get chosen. They must have thousands of applicants."

"So why are we even trying?" Tyler was no fan of doing things without a purpose and especially this. He still wasn't sure he wanted to enter and the idea of doing a video for no reason seemed silly.

"Because there's a chance you could get picked." Nancy pleaded at him with her eyes. "And because it would be so amazing if you got chosen. I could say I know a celebrity. I've always wanted to do that. Please, do it for me." She tilted her head and batted her eyes at him.

Tyler chuckled. It appeared to mean more to Nancy than it did to him. Besides, as Nancy had stated, the chances of him being chosen were slim to none, so why not record the video to make her happy? "Okay, fine," he said holding up his hands in surrender, "what do I need to do?"

Her eyes lit up and she clasped her hands together like a kid on Christmas morning. "Yay, thank you. It's super easy. We need you to tell a little about yourself and what kind of woman you are looking for. I'll go get my phone and we can record it on that."

As Nancy dashed out of the room, Aaron turned to Tyler. "Thanks for this, man. I know it isn't really your cup of tea, but I think you might have made her year."

"My cup of tea?" Tyler couldn't resist teasing his friend, and he picked up his cup deliberately holding out his pinkie. "You need a guy's night out. Nancy's really rubbing off on you."

Aaron rolled his eyes. "It's just a phrase, but a guy's night out sounds good. Let's do it soon."

"Yeah, after I take care of this video. You owe me, by the way. Or maybe Nancy does."

Nancy returned then, her cell phone in hand. Her eyes scanned the room squinting as if searching for the perfect spot. She smiled and pointed to the wall adorned with pictures. "Let's do it there. Give you some contrast."

Tyler stood and walked over to where she was pointing. "Here?"

Her nose wrinkled as she looked at him, and she shook her head. "No, too busy. Can you take two steps to your left?" She motioned with her right hand. "Perfect. Okay, I'll count down and point to you when it's recording. You just state your name, a little about you, and what you are looking for."

He waited until he saw her finger point at him, and then he began speaking. "Uh, hi, my name is Tyler Hall. I own a farm and cattle ranch here in Texas. I'm a Christ follower and looking for a woman who is the same. In addition, I need a woman okay with living in a small town, maybe one looking for a simpler life than the city can provide. I like movies and dancing and riding horses, and I guess that's it." He paused for a second waiting for her to lower the phone. "Is that good?"

"It's perfect," she said with a smile. "Now you need to do the survey."

He followed her over to their small office where she had already loaded the survey questions on her computer. At least this might be interesting. Stretching out in the comfy black leather chair, he leaned back and perused the first question. 'Do you prefer blonds, brunettes, or redheads?' Tyler had no preference, but he was typically more attracted to blonds. A click next to that option moved the screen forward. 'Blue, green, brown, or hazel eyes?' Tyler cared even less about this, and he wondered if all the questions would be about appearance. Question three: 'Are you open to dating a woman outside of your race?' Well, he had never thought about it, but he wasn't opposed.

After a few more questions regarding a contestant's outer appearance, he finally reached the questions with more meat. 'Would your ideal woman enjoy the beach or the mountains more?' He enjoyed both, but he guessed he liked the mountains a little more. 'Would your ideal woman be religious?' That was a tricky question. There was a big difference between being a believer and being religious, but he answered yes anyway. He certainly wanted no one opposed to religion.

He took nearly an hour, but finally he finished the last question. Then Nancy took over uploading the video and sending it out into cyberspace. "There. All done." She turned off the computer and smiled at him. "Now we have to wait."

He was no stranger to waiting though he doubted they'd be waiting for anything but a rejection letter.

5

Laney took a deep breath before knocking on the door. It was nice to be home. There was a warmth and a feeling of security that resided here, and she could use that right now. She'd run away after high school and avoided coming home as often as she could, but it wasn't because of her family. In fact, she'd missed her mother. A lot.

The door swung open and her mother's shocked expression morphed into a giant grin before she pulled Laney in for a hug. "Laney? You're here."

"I am," Laney said with a shrug as she stepped fully into the living room and shut the door behind her.

"I can't believe it. You haven't been home in ages. Your work must keep you so busy." Though said lightly, the words carried a slight disproving tone which Laney chose to ignore.

"It does or did. Madame Bonavich fired me this week."

Laney hated saying the words, hating admitting failure, but her mother would have gotten them out of her eventually. It was one of her mother's specialties. She pulled secrets out of people like they were hanging threads. Visible and just waiting to be unraveled.

"Fired? What on earth for?"

"I was late with her coffee and then spilled it when an intern ran into me. She doesn't tolerate mistakes."

Laney's mother's eyes softened. "That sounds like a terrible place to work. Maybe it's a good thing you got fired."

"Uh yeah." Laney didn't really see getting fired as a good thing in any scenario, but she couldn't deny that she'd slept better the last few nights knowing she no longer had to deal with Madame Bonavich. No more Sunday errands or four-inch-high heels. "Is my room still available?"

Her mother's bottom lip folded under the top one and her eyes shifted to the side. "Well, it's not quite the same. You haven't been home in a while, remember?"

Laney didn't think her mother meant the words as a criticism, but they felt that way nonetheless. She had probably earned them though. She had moved away right out of high school and rarely come home during college. Laney then worked for a modeling agency in Houston for a few years until Myra offered her the job with Madame Bonavich. Once she'd moved to New York, she hadn't been home since. Until now. "Is there at least a bed still?"

Her mother flashed a crooked smile. "Sort of." She continued down the hall to the bedrooms and opened the door that used to be Laney's room. It had been transformed it into a sewing room. Rows of shelves stocked full of colorful fabric and other accoutrements lined the walls where posters of her heartthrobs used to hang. A sewing machine sat where her bed had been, and a futon was the only semblance of a place to lie down.

"Well, I guess it will have to do." Laney tried to keep her voice light but a trickle of hurt coursed through her veins. She shouldn't care about her old room. After all, she was nearing thirty, she had moved away, and she rarely came home. It would be ridiculous to expect them to keep her room for her, and her mother had always wanted a dedicated sewing room.

"The futon is comfortable," her mother said as a way of apology. "I've fallen asleep there quite a few times when I tire of sewing. I always mean to just close my eyes for a bit, but when I wake up, it's a few hours later."

Laney dropped her bag on the futon. "It's fine, Mother. I'll probably only be here for a week or so anyway." With nothing more to do in this room and no real place to sit, Laney headed back toward the kitchen.

"Are you still going back to New York even with no job?" her mother asked following her.

"Not to New York. My friend, Maryanne, whom you left the message about, offered me a makeup job in California for a few weeks, so I'm heading there first. After that," Laney shrugged and pulled out a barstool. "I'm not sure yet. I don't know what the future holds right now."

She plucked an apple from the bowl in the center of the island bar and turned it over in her hands.

"Tea?" Her mother asked, and Laney nodded. "What about marriage?" Her mother said as she plugged in the electric kettle. The words were said carefully and away from Laney, but the scheming inflection in them was undeniable.

The hair on the back of Laney's neck stood at attention. "What about marriage what?" Laney's words were cautious. Who knew what the intent behind her mother's question was.

Her mother turned, an expression that said she had something up her sleeve on her face. "You do want to get married right?"

"Yes, one day, but why do I have the feeling you aren't talking about one day?"

"Okay, don't be mad, but I kind of did something."

Now tiny goosebumps prickled down her back in addition to the raised hairs. "What did you do, Mother?"

"My friend Nadine has this son- "

Laney groaned and dropped her head into her hands. "Oh no, tell me you didn't."

"Well, I want grandchildren, and you always seemed too busy to date. I thought a set up date might help. Of course I didn't know when you might get here, so it's sort of a future set up date, but I could call her and let her know you're in town."

"Mom, I'm about to go to California for six weeks. I don't want to get involved with anyone before I go."

"Okay, but at least consider it when you get back." Her mother crossed to the cabinets and pulled out two ceramic mugs.

"I'll consider it, but I don't even know where I'll be when this show wraps up."

"What show is it?" The pantry opened, and two tea bags appeared in her mother's hand.

"Some reality show, Marry me a Cowboy or something."

Her mother's eyes lit up. "Do you mean Who Wants to Marry a Cowboy?"

"Yeah, I guess so." Her mother's reaction was surprising. She had never been much of a television watcher when Laney lived at home.

"Nadine and I love that show." She dropped the bags in the mugs. "The cowboy always seems like the nicest guy, and he's so handsome. You'll be doing his makeup?" That glint was back in her eye.

"Yes, I'll be doing his makeup."

"Maybe he'll fall in love with you. Wouldn't that be a surprise?" The tea kettle whistled, and her mother turned it off and poured water into the mugs/

"Mom, I don't even like cowboys. I'm a city girl, remember?"

She placed a mug in front of Laney. "You've never dated a cowboy, so how would you know?"

"I've never dated a convict either, but I'm pretty sure I wouldn't enjoy that." Her mother shot her a withering look as she pulled out the opposite barstool and sat down.

"Are you happy with where your life is now?"

Laney opened her mouth to answer, but the thought forced her to pause. Was she happy? She'd attended a college far away to start over. She'd studied makeup design hoping to spice up her image so men might notice her more. Then she'd moved to the Big Apple and dated men in suits who had drivers. None of that made her happy, and now she was single, jobless, and back home.

"No, I guess not, but the man is there to meet beautiful women not fall in love with his makeup artist. Besides, even if I liked this cowboy, he probably wouldn't like me. Most men don't. As much as I've tried to get past it, I'm still *just* Brainy Laney." Brainy Laney. She hated that nickname, but it's how she thought of herself.

She had earned the nickname in middle school when she'd received a valedictorian award.

At first, Laney had been so proud of it as she'd always worked hard for her grades, but then one of the popular boys, Tyson Becker, had begun calling her Brainy Laney. Her mother had insisted that it was because he liked her, but Laney doubted that. Tyson got the nickname to stick and it had followed her into and through high school. That, combined with her girl next door image, had been enough to keep her out of the dating pool in high school. No one had even asked her to prom. Either year. She was everyone's friend, but no one's love interest. She'd hoped learning the art of make-up would change that, but it hadn't seemed to yet.

Her mother's eyes crinkled in sympathy. "Oh honey,

you aren't *just* anything. Certainly not just Brainy Laney. Look at what you've accomplished."

Laney snorted and looked down into her mug. "Yeah, I got fired. Big accomplishment."

"No, I mean look at everything else. You were working for one of the biggest names in New York. You are an amazing makeup artist, and now you will get to show off your work."

"I don't even know if they'll put my name in the credits," Laney said, "and even if they do, it might not mean much. Madame Bonavich didn't let her assistants do makeup until they had worked with her a year. Few ever made it that long."

"I say you forget about Madame Bonavich. You got fired for a reason and this show obviously has something to do with that, so go enjoy yourself and see what doors open afterwards."

Laney watched the light glint off the liquid in her mug. It rippled as if stirred by magic. And maybe it was. Being around her mother always felt a little magical. Laney had often thought her mother a little like Glenda the good witch from The Wizard of Oz when she'd been younger. She looked up with a smile. "You're right, Mom. I'm going to have fun seeing my old friend and take whatever God sends my direction."

6

Tyler flipped through the envelopes hoping not to find a bill. He hadn't made as much with this last trade as he'd been hoping to, and he had no more in the bank. Ad, ad, junk, junk. Wait, what was this?

A plain white envelope with his name hand addressed on it caught his eye. He slid his finger under the back flap and tore the envelope open. Inside was a single sheet of paper. His eyes glanced over it as he unfolded it, and then they bulged. They had chosen him as the bachelor on Who Wants to Marry a Cowboy? But that wasn't possible. He had entered as a joke. Well, not exactly a joke. Maybe on a whim was a better qualifier. On a whim for Nancy. Still, he'd never actually expected them to pick him. Yet, they had, and being the cowboy paid. The amount listed in this letter would be enough to get him out of debt. At least for the rest of this year. All that remained was meeting the producers and signing the contract, at least according to this letter.

He wasn't currently seeing anyone, not since Sierra, so he wouldn't have to worry about that. And it wasn't like he wasn't trying, but he lived in a small town. He was a cowboy who worked a farm and herded cattle. And he didn't have a six-figure bank account. His last few girlfriends had made it abundantly clear they needed more excitement and more financial security in their life.

But a contract? He wondered what it might entail. Silence probably. Though not extremely knowledgeable on the reality show aspect, he assumed one couldn't share the result until after the show ended. That didn't really matter to him - he had no social media presence and rarely shared his business with anyone other than Aaron - but he wondered if he would *have* to marry a woman. He knew that was the point of the show, but what if he felt nothing for any of the women they picked? Or what if he proposed and then found out the woman was nothing like she'd portrayed herself? Would they force him to continue with the marriage for ratings?

Maybe Aaron would know and if not Aaron, then Nancy. She was the one who had gotten him into this after all. Tyler glanced up at the clock on the wall. Dinner time, but Nancy had told him he was always welcome for dinner. Perhaps he could take her up on that offer and get the information he sought. Before he could change his mind, he tucked the letter in his pocket, grabbed his hat and keys, and headed out the door.

Ten minutes later, he turned off the ignition and stepped out of the truck. Aaron and Nancy lived on a ranch twice as large as his. A sprawling split-level home with a wraparound porch sat at the edge of their large property. Tyler envied the porch just a little. His mother had always been fond of them growing up, and one day he hoped to add one to his own modest house. He raised his hand and knocked on their cheery green door.

"Tyler? Well, to what do we owe this pleasure?" Nancy asked as she opened the door. Her brown hair was pulled back in its usual ponytail and she wore a flannel shirt and jeans, her favorite outfit from what he could tell because other than when he saw her in church, he never saw her in anything else.

"Do I need a reason, Nancy?" Tyler flashed his most charming smile.

"Of course not." She stepped back allowing him entrance into the spacious living room. "Come on in. Aaron is grilling burgers out back."

He stepped over the threshold and removed his hat. His hands gripped the fur-based felt brim, curling it slightly. The beat of his heart thudded in his head, and he shook the sound away. He was acting like he was about to ask out a school crush instead of voicing an embarrassing question to his best friend's wife. "Thanks, but uh I have something I wanted to ask you."

"Oh?" She cocked an eyebrow at him before turning and leading the way into the kitchen.

"Yeah, um, you watch those dating reality shows a lot,

right?" Why was this so hard to ask? His throat felt as dry as the Sahara Desert. Man, this felt even more embarrassing than it had when he had played the scene in his head. The brim of his hat curled even tighter in his nervous grip.

"I do." A coy smile flashed across her face as she leaned against the counter. "Why do you ask?"

"Well, you know that video we did a few weeks ago?"

"Uh huh." She wasn't going to let him off the hook easy.

He cleared his throat and forced the remaining words out. "Yeah, well I uh wondered if you knew about the process. What's involved I mean."

"Why? Did you get picked?" Her eyes twinkled, and the pitch of her voice rose at the end of her question. It was clear she already knew they had chosen him.

"Yeah, I did." His gaze dropped to the floor. If he couldn't handle the way she was looking at him now, how was he going to handle the viewing nation looking at him?

A shrill squeal escaped her mouth as she clasped her hands together and did a little jig. "I knew it. I knew you would get picked. You guys didn't believe me, but I knew."

Tyler cleared his throat again. "Right, well, there's a contract involved, and I wondered if you knew what it entailed."

Nancy's smile faltered as her eyes grew serious. "I don't, but I'm sure it won't be anything crazy. You are going to do it, aren't you?"

Tyler paused. He hadn't decided yet, but staring at her

hopeful face, he felt like he should, and he could use the money. And really what could it hurt? As long as he didn't *have* to marry a woman if the chemistry wasn't right, then he might as well throw his hat in the ring. Maybe he would even get lucky and find the perfect woman.

"I suppose I will." She opened her mouth, more than likely to squeal again, but Tyler held up his hand to stop her. "As long as the contract is decent."

"Oh my gosh, I'm so excited. I'm going to call Helen."

Tyler shook his head as Nancy ran off and he continued to the back deck. He wasn't sure he would ever understand women. It was a reality show. Not like they'd cast him in a blockbuster movie or anything.

As Tyler slid open the sliding glass door, Aaron looked up and smiled. "Hey, man, what are you doing over here? You smell the burgers from your house?" Aaron stood by a large circular barbecue grill. Though gas grills were all the rage these days, Aaron claimed he preferred charcoal and therefore he still had a behemoth of a grill. Tyler had to agree that the charcoal made the meat taste better. At least in his head. Who knew if it was just psychosomatic.

"Had to come show you this." He pulled the letter out of his pocket and handed it to his friend.

Aaron took it, a quizzical expression on his face. His eyes widened though as he scanned the paper. "For real? They chose you?"

"Hey now." Tyler feigned a hurt look.

"I just mean that video wasn't anything special. It must be your charm and magnetism. So, you gonna do it?"

"I don't know. Does it make me seem desperate? I mean that's what I think when I hear about these shows." Tyler took the letter back and folded it back into his pocket.

Aaron shrugged. "A little, I guess, but look at it this way, they will find a bunch of women you would never meet and bring them to you. They'll pay for a ton of dates, and they pay you. A lot. Worst case, you have some fun and people recognize you on the streets for a time. Best case, you find the love of your life and finally start that family you've been wanting."

That was true. Tyler supposed it was weird he talked about having a family, but ever since his parents had split and his brother had disowned the family, it had been all he could think about. Unfortunately, his track record with women was atrocious. About the time he started falling for a woman to the point where he could think about proposing, she left him for a more successful man or a more exciting atmosphere. A lawyer, a doctor, one had even left him for an insurance salesman claiming she needed the security his money could offer. Perhaps it was time for him to try something different.

"I guess you're right. Won't find out until you try, right?"

"Indeed. Hungry?" And just like that Aaron dropped the topic, but it didn't fade from Tyler's mind. The meeting with the producers was in a week. He would have to decide by then, and he would have to spend some real time in prayer to make sure this was God's will.

7

Laney pressed her face to the window as the car pulled into the compound. A massive house loomed in front of them. "Is that where we're staying?"

Maryanne laughed as she drove past the house. "No, that is for the women, but it's not as big as it looks. I mean it is, but the women have to share bedrooms and bathrooms. Our accommodations are a little smaller, but we have our own rooms and bathrooms, and the studio pays for the food."

"I'm sure they will be fine. My apartment in New York was tiny. It could have fit in your old living room."

Maryanne glanced her direction. "How did you live in such a small place?"

Laney chuckled. Maryanne had always been a little naïve and evidently, she had not outgrown it. "It was New

York, Maryanne. Everything is small and expensive unless you're a billionaire. Then it's just large and expensive."

"Well, then this might feel like a vacation house after all." She pulled up in front of a row of bungalow type houses surrounding a larger house in the middle. "Our houses are the smaller bungalows. The middle house is for the cowboy, but we also have a meeting room and viewing room in the main house as well as access to the kitchen and our own dining room."

"Wow, this is an impressive set up. Does the studio own all this?"

"Yeah, they film here nine months out of the year, so it made sense to just buy it. Our show isn't the only show that uses it." She parked the car in front of the main house. "Come on inside. I'll show you your room and then introduce you to everyone."

Laney grabbed her suitcases from the trunk of the car. Maryanne had insisted she didn't need much as they had a laundry on site and Laney would have time to drive into town to get whatever else she might need, but Laney didn't feel comfortable going somewhere for more than a month without enough clothes. Not knowing what exactly she was getting into, she'd packed for every occasion and barely gotten her suitcase closed. Her second suitcase contained only her makeup supplies.

"Let's drop your suitcases off first." Maryanne led the way to the right of the main building stopping at the second bungalow. "I'm in number one and our cook,

Reynaldo, is in number three. You have lucky number two."

Two had never been Laney's lucky number, but she said nothing as Maryanne pulled a ring of keys from her pocket and unlocked the door before handing the key to Laney. The door opened to a small but spacious living room which held a couch, a chair, and a small table.

"No television?" Laney asked as she looked around the room.

"No, we're not supposed to watch anything except what plays in the group space but believe me that is entertaining as it's a live feed of the women. There are cameras all over the place in this compound, so be careful what you do. Oh, that reminds me, I'll have to take your phone too."

Laney's mouth dropped open. "My phone? But it has all my books on it."

"Don't worry," Maryanne said with a smile. "You can use it in the common space, just not in your bungalow. It's part of the contract you'll have to sign. They don't want any leaking of the show."

Laney's eyes narrowed at her friend. "I guess there are a few things you forgot to mention when you told me about this gig." Honestly, Laney didn't mind though. Her phone had always been glued to her side when she worked for Madame Bonavich. The woman could and often had called at all times of the day and night. Laney was rather looking forward to a detox from her phone.

Maryanne's bottom lip folded under her teeth in a

contrite expression. She looked like a kid who'd gotten caught with her hand in the cookie jar. "I know and I'm sorry, but I needed you to take the job. I promise I'll make it up to you."

"You bet you will." Laney laughed to let her friend know she was teasing. She continued toward the back of the room where it opened to a small hallway with two doors. One held a bathroom and the other a bedroom. Simple - just a bed, nightstand, dresser, and closet, but it would do, and even though it wasn't large, it was bigger than her apartment had been.

After hoisting her suitcase on the bed to unpack later, she followed Maryanne out of the bungalow and toward the main house.

"We always enter from back here where the kitchen is. There's a separate dining room for us back here and one for the cowboy up front. Our goal is to stay out of his sight as much as possible. Of course, you'll have to be around him more than the rest of us, but that's unavoidable. Still, as you'll find out in a minute, it's get in, do his makeup, and get out. As little interaction as possible."

"Got it. Is there a reason?"

Maryanne opened the back door and motioned Laney inside. A spacious kitchen lay before them, but Laney hardly had time to take it all in before Maryanne was moving again. "He's supposed to be focusing on the women to find a wife." She glanced around and then leaned closer to Laney. "They hardly ever last, but the producers like to think they will if the contestants focus enough. So, we give them as much space as we can."

The kitchen led out to a dining room that held a table for eight, but Maryanne kept walking. "How many shows have there been?" Laney should have done more homework. She was all kinds of curious now.

"This is our tenth season."

Laney blinked. "Wow, ten seasons. I had no idea. How many matches have lasted?"

"Only one, but that's hardly surprising since they only get to know each other a few weeks before the end of the show. They almost always end in a proposal but there's only been one wedding."

Laney's eyes widened. "That's a terrible record. Why do people keep coming on the show?"

Maryanne shrugged as she stopped in front of a closed door. "A myriad of reasons but mostly to get their fifteen minutes of fame. Okay, this is the conference room. Peter, the director, and Justin, the host, are probably inside already. They'll give you the contract to sign. I'll answer any questions you have later, but don't bring up the success rate to them." Her mouth twitched, and she glanced around covertly. "They're kind of touchy about it."

"Got it." Laney wondered just what she had gotten herself into. She'd thought it was simply a reality television show, but already it felt like a different world.

Two men looked up at them as the door opened. One was older, probably in his late fifties or early sixties if the gray in his hair was any indication. The other looked younger, maybe mid-thirties, but it was hard to tell. He had to be the host though as he looked like what Laney imagined a Ken doll would if one came to life. Blond hair that laid in a perfect wave on his head, a pronounced cleft in his chin, and a smile that shifted between plastic and predatory.

"Peter, Justin, this is Laney, the makeup artist I told you about."

Justin's eyes roamed over her briefly and then shifted away. Perhaps she didn't meet his standard of approval but that was fine with her as he appeared narcissistic and closed off. Peter, however, stood and extended a hand.

"Laney, it's a pleasure to meet you, and I can't thank you enough for coming on such short notice. I thought our normal girl would make it through filming, but she had complications with her pregnancy and the doctors forced her to start maternity leave early."

"I hope she's okay." A surge of concern flooded Laney though she didn't know this woman and would probably never meet her.

Peter waved a hand. "She's fine, but she's having twins and I guess her amniotic fluid was low. I'm not even sure what that means, but she's on bedrest, so here we are."

While low amniotic fluid held some risks, Laney was glad to hear it was something relatively minor. "I'm glad to hear she'll be okay and happy I could help."

"Good, good. Take a seat and I'll fill you in on the basic contract. Maryanne can answer any other questions you have. So, first and foremost, you can't discuss the show and how it's going. Obviously, we don't film live and we don't want details getting leaked. You'll have a locker in the viewing area where you can leave your phone and computer if you have one. There's no Wi-Fi in the house anyway, but we monitor all your online activity. If you leak information, it is grounds for termination."

Laney tried hard not to focus on the word termination. She'd been fired from one job this month, she had no desire to lose another. "Understood."

"You are responsible for his makeup and attire every day he goes on a date. Not that you must dress him, but you need to make sure what he is wearing will work well on the HD cameras, and if not, then help him pick something that will. You will probably need to go on most dates in case he needs a touchup, but you can either wait in the car or sit with Maryanne. However, because you'll have such a bird's-eye view of everything, it is important that you don't influence his decision."

"Right, I think I can handle that."

"Good, then you just need to sign here." He slid a single sheet of paper her direction. Laney scanned it - she had learned never to sign anything without reading it - but the contract covered just what he'd gone over. She didn't see any surprises in it, so she took the proffered pen and signed her name to the bottom.

"Welcome to the family," Peter said and extended his hand one more time.

8

"What took so long?" Laney asked as she took the cup. She kept her voice low and glanced around at the other crew members. "You're cutting it pretty close."

Maryanne shrugged. "The machine had a problem. You'll get used to that. Justin seems to be the only who can make it work consistently. I could have gone off the compound, but I didn't want to risk being late and leaving you all alone."

"Thanks, I appreciate that." Though Laney had met most of the crew, she still felt like the outsider. "And thanks for the coffee. I was up way too late last night."

"Hot date?" Maryanne asked with a wink.

"Hardly." The word escaped Laney's mouth more as a snort than a word. She'd unpacked and then lain in bed unable to sleep as she tried to figure out what she wanted out of life after this show. "First of all, I have no car, so who exactly would I have gone on a date with?"

Maryanne glanced to the front left and indicated with her head. "Justin's available." She said the words with a serious tone, but the smile that tugged on the corners of her mouth betrayed her.

"No thank you," Laney said. "Besides, men don't seem to want the girl next door. They want a Jennifer Lopez or Kim Kardashian type of woman, and I am definitely not that."

"Don't sell yourself short. You are beautiful and one day you'll meet the right man."

Laney scoffed. "Easy for you to say. You've already found your Prince Charming." Maryanne had filled her in on everything Laney had missed in the last decade including her marriage to a renowned cardiac surgeon. It seemed there was a man out there for everyone except her. She was trying to be patient and wait on God's timing, but it certainly wasn't easy.

The door opened, and Peter stepped in. He scanned the room as if doing a visual count - it wasn't hard as the crew was small - nodded and then began to speak. "Great, it looks like everyone is here. I decided it would be nice for you all to meet our cowboy. He comes from the great state of Texas where he owns a farm and cattle ranch."

The door opened, and a man stepped in. Dark hair peeked from beneath a black cowboy hat and when he removed it, Laney saw cool blue eyes. Her breath caught as he stepped closer to Peter. His chiseled features seemed almost etched from stone, but he didn't appear fierce. Far from it. He looked masculine yet… Soft wasn't the right word, but like someone you could share secrets with.

And instead of seeming cocky as she had expected, he seemed embarrassed to be there and facing them all. A light pink color graced his cheeks and his eyes shifted from them to the floor. "Hi, everybody. I'm Tyler Hall, and I guess I'm your new Cowboy."

"How on earth is this man single?" Laney whispered to Maryanne. "He's gorgeous."

Maryanne's eyebrow lifted. "Two possibilities. One, for the same reason you are. He hasn't found the right person yet or two, and probably more likely, he needs money or recognition for something. Maybe his ranch."

"They pay them?"

"Only him. It isn't usually much but as I said, most do it hoping to appear on another show after."

So, he was getting paid. Somehow Laney couldn't imagine this man doing it just for the fame or the money though. He looked too uncomfortable. Besides, there was a wholesome honest look to his face, and she guessed there was another reason behind his acceptance.

"Tyler, I'll introduce you to everyone in a minute, but now that you're here, I'll give a rundown of the show. The women will be arriving tonight. Twenty of them. We'll be filming the first few weeks here. Cameras are in the house and run twenty-four seven. We don't always use that footage, but it's nice to have. Plus, we'll film a date episode every few days. Those air every week on Mondays and

Tuesdays, so most of the people you see here will be the editing team working around the clock to make sure those episodes are ready. Justin will monitor the focus group who sees the episodes first to see if the audience doesn't connect with certain women or believes that others should have more time. Generally, we take the top four contestants back to the cowboy's house to meet his family and friends. The final episode, with the proposal, will be filmed there if Tyler has no objection."

"No objection from me," Tyler said. "I want a woman who doesn't mind a ranch life so it's important for them to see it."

Laney wondered what a ranch life entailed. She'd only known the city life though the few movies she'd seen set in the country had held a certain appeal. When Peter finished his spiel, he began taking Tyler around introducing him to the crew. Laney figured she had enough time to drain the last of her coffee and sneak the stick of gum she had in her pocket before they reached her and Maryanne. He might be off limits, but there was no reason to spew coffee breath on the man when she met him. She tipped back her cup and sighed. All gone. She'd have to ask Maryanne how to work the machine later, so she could make herself some more. "Are you done? I'll go throw these away." Laney wiggled her cup at Maryanne to indicate what she meant.

"Sure, thank you."

Maryanne handed over her cup, and Laney made her way toward the door where the trash can sat but before she reached the corner, her foot caught on the leg of a chair pushed back just a little too far. The cups flew out of her hands as her body fell forward and a little to the right. She expected to smack the concrete floor, but she didn't hit the ground. Instead strong arms enveloped her, and she found herself staring up into Tyler's face. Tyler's handsome, chiseled, strong face. Oh gracious, he had the most amazing blue eyes. Dark like sapphires.

"Easy there. You okay?"

His voice broke through her stare, and she realized her hands were splayed across his chest - his muscular, solid chest. Heat burned up her neck, and she knew her ears were probably blazing beacons of her attraction to him.

"Sorry, I, uh guess I should pay more attention to where I'm walking." She tried to extricate herself from his arms as gracefully as possible in hopes that no one else had seen the spectacle and she wouldn't become the laughingstock of the crew.

"And here I thought you were just falling for me." His eyes twinkled as he grinned at her, and Laney's knees turned to jelly. "I don't believe we've met. I'm Tyler Hall." He held out his hand for a shake. Laney hoped her palm was dry and not the sweaty mess she feared it was as she placed her hand in his. His face didn't shift into one of disgust which gave Laney the courage to speak.

"I'm Laney Swann, your makeup artist." Her voice came out scratchy and quiet, but she resisted the urge to clear her throat. She didn't want to belay her nervousness any more than she already had.

"I have a makeup artist?" He blinked at her. "Do I need one?"

Laney had no idea if he were serious or simply fishing for a compliment. "Um, well, it's more about making sure you look good on the cameras. HD picks up everything."

His eyes bore into hers sending a tingle down her spine. "Well, I guess I'll be seeing more of you in the future."

"Yep, every day." Oh geez, she sounded like some giddy school girl. She clamped her mouth shut to keep from spewing any more nonsense at the man.

He held her gaze another moment before Peter called him back over to introduce him to the editing team. Laney let out a breath and made her way back to Maryanne. She kept her head down, but she could feel the heat clawing up her neck.

"What was that about?" Maryanne asked with a raised eyebrow as Laney sat.

"What do you mean?"

"I mean you looked like a star-struck fan down there. Your face was all flushed. I haven't seen you look like that since Dallas."

"Oh goodness." Laney dropped her head in her hands. "Was I that obvious?"

Maryanne giggled. "How could it not be obvious? You practically swan dived into his arms. You better be careful, or you might end up a contestant yourself."

Laney groaned into her hands. "I didn't mean to. He should have just let me fall. This is so embarrassing. Of course, I would have to be rescued before he even knows me. I can't believe I'm going to have to be working so close to him."

"Not to mention watching him go on dates to find a wife."

Another groan billowed forth. Yes, there was that; she had forgotten about that fact momentarily. "Don't remind me. I'm beginning to think this was a very bad idea."

TYLER'S EYES followed the pretty blond the rest of the meeting. She wasn't one of his contestants, but he couldn't deny the surge of electricity that had shot through his arms when he'd caught her. And her eyes. There was something about them that stuck in his mind. A vulnerability he not only wanted to explore but also wanted to protect, but that was silly. He didn't even know the woman.

"I saw that you met Laney, our new girl, but let me introduce you to Maryanne, one of our main camera operators," Peter said leading the way to the two women.

The red had disappeared from Laney's face, but she kept her eyes averted from his as Peter introduced him to the Korean woman next to her. Was that from embarrassment or had she felt something too?

"I'm Maryanne. It's a pleasure to meet you, Tyler. I'll be filming the dates, so I guess I'll get to see a lot of you."

"Looking forward to it," he said shaking her hand.

"All right, that's all the crew, but let me show you around the place and then you can get settled in for a few hours before Laney comes to do your makeup. Are you ready to meet the women?"

"I suppose I will be in a few hours."

"Great. I think you'll really like the women we found for you. They come from all walks of life, but they matched your personality questions." Peter continued talking as he led Tyler around the compound and then finally to his space.

The simple main room held just a table and a few chairs, and a single hallway led back to a bedroom with an attached bath. Nothing extreme but nice. It wasn't home, but Tyler thought it would be a suitable replacement for a few weeks.

9

Tyler stared up at Laney as she poured liquid foundation into a spray bottle. "What is that?"

"This?" she held up the bottle. "This is an air brush machine. You've heard of it, right?"

"Yeah, but I thought they airbrushed pictures for magazines. I didn't realize they airbrushed people."

A tiny smile pulled at the corners of her mouth. It was a cute, lopsided smile. "They do airbrush magazine pictures, but they also airbrush people for TV. HD is wicked. It will pick up every pore in your face."

He ran a hand across his chin as if searching for gaping holes. "Do I have big pores for it to find?"

She chuckled and shot him a look out of the corner of her eye as she screwed the lid back on the machine. "Not really, but they want you to appear perfect, so-" she shrugged letting the words fade away. "Close your eyes, please."

He shut his eyes and took a deep breath as the motor on the air brush machine whirred to life. A breath of air covered his face moving slowly left to right. It didn't feel much like makeup, but he'd never worn any before, so he had nothing to compare it to.

The motor stopped, and he opened his eyes. "Am I beautiful now?"

A pink blush graced her cheeks. "I might use the word dashing, but yes, almost." She set the air brush down and picked up a small plastic tool with a comb-like head.

"Dashing, huh? I haven't heard that word in a while." In fact, no one he knew had used that word since his grandmother who used to always tell him he looked dashing when he wore his suits for church. "Are you from around here?"

She shook her head and moved the brush across his eyebrows. Her face was close enough he noticed a tiny dimple in her left cheek and the smattering of freckles that dusted her nose. "Texas originally, but I've been living in New York for the past six months."

"Texas?" His head perked up at the mention of home and the finding of a kindred spirit out in this foreign place. "What part?"

"Houston where it's hot and humid. How about you?"

"Frederiksberg. The good ole Peach of Texas." They might both be from the Lone Star State, but that was where the similarities ended. She was a city girl and he preferred the country.

"I can't say I've ever been there, but I do love peaches." Laney's lips pursed as she stepped back and looked him over. It was an odd experience as she looked at him more like a piece of art than a person. "Okay, I think you're ready."

His heart sped up in his chest as his nerves pulled taut. "Are you sure? I don't need any more touch ups?"

Her brow furrowed, and she shook her head. "You said you didn't want makeup, and now you want more?"

"Actually, I'm just nervous about meeting these women. I'm not generally a limelight kind of guy."

"Kind of hard to avoid when you agree to the be the bachelor on a reality dating show. If you didn't want the limelight why did you do it?" She began packing up her supplies, but the tilt of her head told him she was still listening.

"My friend's wife is very persuasive."

Laney turned back to him. "What, did she obtain some dirty laundry on you?"

"No, she's just an amazing cook, and I didn't want her banning me from dinner. After my last girlfriend broke up with me, she suggested this. I didn't think I'd get chosen though."

"I can see why they chose you." Her eyes held his for a moment and then she turned away, but not before he saw the blush climb her face once again.

An awkward silence descended. Tyler felt the need to say something, but he didn't know what. He didn't know her, not really, and they would have to work together for the next few weeks. "Right, well I guess I better get out there. Wish me luck."

"Good luck," Laney said, but she kept her face turned from him.

Tyler hoped he hadn't made her uncomfortable, but he couldn't worry about that now. Right now, he had to put on his game face, meet twenty women, and pretend this whole thing didn't scare him out of his mind.

TYLER BLINKED AGAINST the blinding lights. How was he supposed to act natural with all the bright light shining in his face?

"Are you ready?" Justin asked.

No, he wasn't ready. Why had he ever thought this would be a good idea? He was in a foreign city, wearing rented clothes and makeup of all things, and waiting for twenty women he had never met who had agreed to come based on his photo and interests alone. "I guess as ready as I'll ever be." It sounded like the worst kind of meat market especially for a small-town rancher hoping for more than a physical attraction.

"You'll do great. Just be yourself." Tyler assumed Justin's words were meant to boost his confidence but as the man put little emotion behind the words, they fell flat on Tyler's ears.

Tyler took the moment to scan the area. Peter sat in a director's chair off to the left, a pair of headphones on his head and a monitor in front of him. A lanky man whose name failed him held a boom mic his direction and Justin stood to the side. A sole camera focused on him a few yards away. Maryanne and Laney sat behind it. Laney flashed him a thumbs up sign when she caught him staring at her. He smiled back and relaxed a little. He could do this.

The sound of a car engine reached his ears and Tyler smoothed his shirt. He adjusted his tie and cleared his throat. It was dry as if he had swallowed a bug, one that refused to be dislodged, but he knew it was just his nerves. A black stretch limo pulled up and the door opened. A blond woman with a skin-tight evening gown stepped out. The slit in her dress went nearly to her hip and the front dipped quite low as well.

Her eyes lit up and her lips stretched to a wide smile as she caught sight of him. He waited as she carefully stepped up the path. She was pretty, but a little too revealing for him. He wanted a more modest woman, but perhaps this was for the camera. Maybe she was more modest normally. He tried to keep an open mind, but when she spoke, the shrillness of her voice told him she wouldn't be the one he chose in the end.

"Oh, my goodness, you're even more handsome than I imagined." Her voice was high and pitchy, almost like Minnie Mouse. "Can I wear your hat?" She reached up and without thinking he took a step back. Didn't she realize it was rude to ask for a cowboy's hat unless you were dating him?

"Sorry, it's covering up my hat hair," he said trying to salvage his reaction.

"Oh, well, maybe later. I'm Stacie by the way. With an IE and not a Y."

Of course, she was. This woman oozed "high maintenance" in every way sense of the word and sent off warning bells in Tyler's head. She was Sierra and the three previous women rolled into one, and he wondered how she had made it past the survey. There was no way he could envision her on his ranch or any ranch. "Well, I look forward to getting to know you better."

Tyler didn't, but they had told him to try to give everyone a fair chance. It was harder than he thought it would be, and he wondered if he would be able to keep a stoic face if the rest of the women were like this. What if he felt nothing for any of them? Would they force him to continue even if it was obvious there was no match for him?

She blinked at him, obviously taken off guard. "Oh, yes. I look forward to getting to know you better as well."

Tyler breathed a sigh of relief as Stacie with an IE walked up the rest of the path and into the house. Surely the next woman would be better. Pulling his shoulders back, he turned back to the limo. They had told him four women would arrive in every limo. The door opened again, and a stunning redhead exited.

Now, she was a little more his style. Beautiful but in an understated way. Her long hair fell in a soft curl about her shoulders and while her evening gown was form fitted, it had a much more modest neckline and much smaller slit. This time there was no need to fake his smile.

"Hello," he said when she reached his side. He held out his hand to her. "I'm Tyler."

She smiled as she took it and looked up at him with these amazing green eyes that seemed to sparkle in the light. "I'm Heidi."

His breath caught a little in his chest. "What do you do Heidi?"

"I'm a preschool teacher in Washington state."

He blinked at her. Washington state. That information stunned Tyler. He supposed he had known these women came from all over the country but hearing her say she lived in a state across the country from him brought home the reality that either he or the woman he chose might have to leave their home and move at the end of this journey.

"Washington state. I can't say I've ever been there."

"It's beautiful if you don't mind the rain. It rains a lot." Her eyes twinkled as her lips pulled into a crooked smile.

"You'll have to tell me more about it." Though he wanted to talk with Heidi longer, they had told him to keep each first meeting to a minute or less. They claimed he would have plenty of time to talk to the women after the initial meeting. He hoped so, but he would have to keep Heidi on his radar.

The next woman to exit was a tall brunette. She wasn't as thin as the other two women, but her athletic build was appealing. He could see her riding horses with him, and he added her to his mental list.

Then a stunning blond exited. She had a bubbly air about her he found appealing, and he wanted to get to know her better as well.

"Let's take a break before the next car," Peter hollered. The lights cut off and Tyler sighed a breath of relief. He had never thought acting was hard, but he felt as if he'd just done a physical workout, and there were four more cars to go.

"Ready for your touch up?" Laney appeared at his side, brush and makeup in hand.

"More?" He hadn't done anything to smear the makeup that he knew of.

"Yep, a touch up. The lights are hot and they're afraid you might have sweated some off, so I have to retouch during every break."

"I guess my face is all yours."

She dipped her brush in some powder and ran it across his face.

"How's it looking?"

"Your face?" She smiled. "It looks good. I'm almost finished."

"No, I don't mean my face. I mean the whole thing. Is my nervousness as apparent as I think it is?" He wasn't sure why he was asking her other than she was the person he had spent the most time with so far, and she had an honest air about her. He held her gaze as he waited for her answer.

"You look fine. Just be yourself." She squeezed his arm, and his eyes fell to her hand. It was nothing, a friendly touch but it sent off a surge of heat in his arm. Before he uttered another word though, she disappeared, and the next limo arrived.

Laney bit her lip as she watched the next limo pull up. This was harder than she'd thought it would be. She shouldn't care what these women looked like or how Tyler reacted to them, but she did. With each one he seemed uninterested in, her heart gave a tiny cheer, but with each one he smiled at, her stomach knotted, and her fists clenched at her side.

"Are you okay?" Maryanne asked as Laney leaned forward to catch Tyler's reaction to the stunning brunette.

"What? Yeah, I'm fine. Just checking to see how his makeup looks in the camera. I want to make sure I do a good job."

Maryanne's eyebrow edged up her forehead. "Uh huh. Look, I get he's good looking, but you can't fall for him, Laney. He's here to marry one of these women."

"I know that."

"You might know that, but you aren't acting like that."

Laney took a deep breath. Maryanne was right. She was here to do a job, and she needed to focus on that.

"Cut."

Peter's voice carried across the lot and Laney picked up

her tools. "That's my cue." Maryanne shot her a pointed stare and Laney nodded. She could do this. She could build up her emotional wall and ignore the tingle that raced through her veins when she was near him. Emotional walls were her specialty after all. *Focus. Do your job and get out. Little interaction, remember?*

"How's it going?" she asked when she reached Tyler. He didn't need a touchup, but she ran the brush across his face anyway.

"It's a little daunting. These women seem great, but how am I going to know who to keep and who to let go?"

Laney bit her lip. *Keep it short and keep it professional.* "I guess you'll have to follow your heart." Easy advice to spout but much harder to take. She certainly wasn't doing that.

"Thanks." He caught her eye and held her gaze. "I appreciate that."

Laney forced a smile to her lips. "No problem. It's what I'm here for… and your makeup obviously. Speaking of which, you're good to go."

As she walked back to Maryanne, she took a deep breath. She could do this, but she needed to get her emotions under control.

"Well, Tyler, you've gotten to meet the women. Do you have any that stand out in your mind?"

Tyler did have a few he really wanted to get to know better, but they had told him to be vague at the beginning. Part of keeping the ratings up was not letting the viewers discern his favorites too soon. The first ceremony would be tonight and that would be their first clue.

"Yeah, a lot of them do, but I must tell you, Justin, it's kind of hard keeping twenty women straight. I am going to get more time with them, right?"

Justin flashed his fake TV smile. "Of course you will. In fact, why don't we head inside now? You can pick the first woman you'd like to talk with one on one."

"And how much time do I get with each woman? "Tyler asked. Even half an hour with each woman would mean ten more hours. He doubted they would film that long, but this was one area they hadn't clarified with him.

Justin's smile froze giving his expression an insincere plastic look. "We'll be having the ceremony in two hours."

"Two hours? How am I supposed to get to know twenty women in two hours? That's not even ten minutes with each one." Tyler's voice held an edge of panic and he forced himself to take a deep breath, but this was his future here. How was he supposed to make the right decision or more importantly keep from making the wrong one with only two hours?

"Cut." Anger filled Peter's voice as he hollered from his chair. "Justin, didn't you go over how he should handle this evening with him?"

Justin's forced smile faded, and he rolled his eyes. "I told him what we always tell them, but you know they always freak out the first night." He turned his attention back to Tyler. "Look, you're only eliminating five tonight. Surely there are five women you didn't connect with."

Tyler's brow furrowed. "There might have been a couple, but I don't know about five. Isn't this supposed to be about finding the right woman though? What if I cut a woman I would have had a connection with but didn't get the chance to know?"

"Look, I've been doing this long enough to know that there are women you didn't have an initial attraction to. Then there are the ones you did. Finally, there are a handful that don't really stand out one way or the other to you. My advice is start with those. Talk with them during these two hours and find out which ones you can let go. Then you'll have more time to get to know the others."

While Justin's advice made sense, Tyler still wasn't happy that he had such a short time with the women. What if they did this again? He didn't like having to make such heavy decisions with so little time. "You promise there will be more time from here on out?"

Justin's eye twitched. "There will be time, but it may never feel like enough. The only thing I can say is use it wisely."

"Are we ready to redo this scene now?" Peter called from the side.

Justin looked at Tyler, his brow raised in a silent question.

"Fine," Tyler said. There wasn't much he could do about it now anyway.

"Take two."

"So, Tyler, you've gotten to meet the women. Do you have any that stand out in your mind?" Justin's game show host smile was back on his face like this was the first time he had asked the question and didn't know the answer. No wonder the guy was snarky in real life. Tyler probably would be too if this was what he had to do.

He wanted to say no. He wanted to ask for his contract right now and maybe rip it to shreds and throw it at Peter, but instead Tyler pasted on his own smile knowing it probably looked about as real as fool's gold. "Absolutely, Justin. I'd like the chance to get to know them all more."

"Well, then let's head inside. This house is where the

women will be staying, but don't worry, we have an apartment just as nice for you."

The house was indeed amazing, and Tyler probably would have enjoyed the view more if he didn't have twenty women staring at him as if he were the last man on earth. He could almost hear claws sharpening as the women looked around at each other. Tyler briefly wondered if they would need a security guard to keep the peace in the house. This many women stuck together seemed dangerous, but this many women stuck together while competing for the same man felt like a recipe for disaster.

"Hello, ladies. How do you like your digs?" Justin spread his arms, gesturing at the room around them.

The women clapped and cheered. One sporty girl Tyler remembered stood and hooted, shaking her arm in a circular manner. Several other girls shot her a withering glance, and he didn't blame them. She wasn't high on his list either and probably wouldn't make it through the night.

"Good, but don't get too comfortable because only fifteen of you will be staying." Justin's smile looked almost genuine as he gazed out at the shocked women. "Tyler is going to get the next two hours to get to know you better. Then we'll have the ceremony. Whoever doesn't get a miniature cowboy hat from Tyler will have to return home."

Evidently the women had not been informed of this little tidbit of information either. Dropped jaws and worried expressions filled the room.

"Who would you like to start with, Tyler?" Justin continued as if he didn't see the women.

Tyler was still processing the women's reactions and his own feelings, so the question caught him off guard. He stared out at the sea of faces not remembering any of their names for a moment. Then his gaze landed on Heidi and Jade and Michelle - all women he wanted to get to know better, but that hadn't been what Justin suggested. Justin had suggested picking the women he wasn't sure about. He continued to scan the faces and landed on the woman he thought worked at the fire department. Cassidy? He found her pretty but wondered if they would have enough in common to form a lasting relationship.

"I'd like to start with Cassidy."

Her eyes lit up and surprise colored her face as she stood and crossed the room to him. Daggers issued from the other women's eyes and Tyler felt certain he had just put a target on Cassidy's back.

"THIS IS when it starts to get interesting," Maryanne whispered to Laney as she scanned the room with the camera. They would have to follow Tyler outside in a minute, but Maryanne had insisted she needed some footage from inside.

"What do you mean?" Laney looked around the room, but other than the lack of furniture and the number of women filling the living room, she saw nothing out of place.

"Notice there's no television. They get their phones taken away when they arrive too."

Realization dawned on Laney, and her eyes widened. "So, they have no entertainment besides each other?"

"And Tyler when he comes around. They have a full bar though."

At that moment, a woman stumbled into the room and called out, "Ya'll there's a pool. Who wants to jump in with me?"

"Oh my gosh, is she drunk already?" Laney couldn't believe any woman would drink enough to get sloshed on the first night of the show, but she supposed nerves played a large role. She didn't know the women's names, but she had begun giving them nicknames based on their looks or actions and this one deserved the name Tipsy from now on.

Maryanne smiled. "Yep, and it only gets better. The bar is open twenty-four hours a day, there are only two bathrooms, and they bunk the women four to a room."

Laney's eyes widened. "Are they trying to get one of these women killed?"

"It rarely gets that far, but it does make for some comedic moments. Come on, we better get outside."

Laney followed Maryanne, but her eyes remained on the women. Now that she knew what she was looking for, she found nearly every woman had a drink in her hand. None looked quite as inebriated as Tipsy, but it was still early, and Laney wasn't sure who she felt sorrier for - the women placed in this awkward position or Tyler who had no idea what was going on in here. She wondered if they would allow him to watch the recorded footage.

Outside there was indeed a pool, and a small gazebo area which was where Tyler and the pretty brunette were sitting now. This one seemed nice, and Laney had a hard time coming up with a name for her. As Maryanne focused the camera, Laney stood to the side and tried to be inconspicuous. It felt awkward being close enough to hear their conversations.

"So, a firefighter, that must keep you busy," Tyler said.

Firefighter, hmm? Then Flame it was.

"It does. It's quite the hectic schedule, but the good news is that it's fairly easy to get a job wherever you go. I love Illinois, don't get me wrong, but I think I could love Texas just as much."

"Do you work in a large city in Illinois?"

Flame shrugged. "Just over a hundred thousand people I guess."

Tyler opened his mouth to respond, but a second brunette cut him off. This one had dark black eyeliner extending like cat eyes. "I believe it's my turn now," Cat Eyes said as she stared at Flame.

"I believe I still have some time," Flame said returning the stare. Laney wasn't a better, but had she been, she would have placed her money on Flame. Cat Eyes was way out of her league.

"It's okay," Tyler broke in, "we can continue this later."

Flame evidently took this as a hint she would be around after the ceremony and gave up her seat. Cat Eyes swooped in and scooted as close to Tyler as she could. Any closer and she would have been in his lap which was probably her goal. "I'm Debra, and I must say you have the most amazing eyes."

Laney turned away from the scene. Being professional didn't mean she had to watch the women fawn all over Tyler. His makeup was fine, so surely, she could take a break for a minute. She signed to Maryanne what she was doing and then walked away from the filming.

11

Tyler stood in the small room staring at the pictures of the women. It was late, and exhaustion covered him, but Justin claimed they had to have the ceremony tonight. He rubbed his bloodshot eyes and took down Stacie with an IE's picture. There was no sense leaving her up there as they would never make a good pair.

And Debra R, he took her down. During his conversation with Cassidy, she had rudely interrupted demanding time with him. As if that wasn't bad enough, she'd been extremely handsy and tried to kiss him. He needed none of that. But that was only two. He needed to trim three more and he honestly didn't know how he would do that. He glanced at his watch. It was after midnight. No wonder his body was so tired. Generally, he was in bed by nine.

He ran a hand across his chin. Okay, maybe it would be easier if he made a pile of those he wanted to keep. Heidi, Jade, Michelle for sure - he had felt a connection with them. Rachel B had seemed nice, Cassidy, and Bristol. Six? Good grief, this would take him all night at this rate.

Tyler scanned the rest of the pictures. Okay there was Nikki, the outspoken sporty one, he removed her and Stephanie - the tipsy one who'd jumped in the pool in her evening gown, but he honestly remembered nothing about the remaining women. He hated judging them by looks alone, but if he didn't, they would probably lock him in the room all night and he still wouldn't have a decision. They just hadn't given him enough time. He removed the woman he was least attracted to, hating himself as he did it, and placed her in the pile with Stacie with an IE, Debra R, Nikki, and Stephanie. Tyler could only hope he would get to know the rest of the women before the next ceremony. He pressed the small button to inform Justin he was ready and waited to be escorted out.

Twenty minutes later, Tyler stood staring out at the sea of women. They all wore hopeful, worried expressions and he hated himself a little more. He was going to hurt five women's feelings, and the thought made him sick. Nancy hadn't warned him about this part, about how hard it would be to dash women's dreams.

"Ladies, you've had some time to get to know Tyler, and he's had a chance to get to know you a little better. There are twenty of you here, but after tonight, only fifteen will remain. Tyler has a stack of miniature hats. He will call your name and offer you a hat. You have the choice to accept it or reject it and leave of your own accord. If you do not receive a hat, you must leave the house immediately and return home. Tyler, when you're ready."

Justin's face held a look of satisfaction and Tyler wondered if he didn't sadistically enjoy this part of his job. Perhaps, he hadn't always been this way. Maybe the show had jaded him. Tyler would have to guard himself, so he didn't end up like Justin, but that was a worry for another night. Tonight, he had to get through this ceremony. He had to hand out these hats to fifteen women and send five others home feeling dejected. Hopefully, the ending would justify his actions tonight.

He took a deep breath and picked up the first hat. It felt light in his hand which was odd considering the weight it carried. "Heidi." Tyler said the name without looking at the women. While he would have liked to see Heidi's smile, he held no desire to see the hurt, angry, fearful faces of the rest of the women.

When Heidi's shoes came into sight, he forced his eyes up, careful to keep them focused on her face and nowhere else. "Heidi, will you accept my hat?"

"I'd be delighted to." She flashed a smile, accepted the token, and then walked to the side.

Tyler picked up the next hat. "Jade." He waited for her to reach him. "Will you stick around a little longer?"

"Of course." She took the hat and walked over to join Heidi.

One after the other, he picked up the hats and handed

them out to women. As the stack dwindled, the tension in the room increased and a trickle of sweat snaked down his back.

"All right ladies, this is the final hat tonight." Justin's voice broke the somber mood momentarily, but as soon as he stepped back, the temperature dropped in the room. The mood shifted from somber to icy. Palpable feelings of hope, rejection, disbelief, and anger circulated through the room, and Tyler had to force himself not to run out of the room.

He picked up the final hat and bit his lip. This one shouldn't bother him so much. All the women he'd felt a connection stood on his left, but this hat held the uncertainty. With this hat, he would send away five women, only four of which he was sure he saw no future with. That left one he was unsure on. What if he sent the wrong woman away? He dared his first glance at the women. One had her eyes closed, a few shot daggers his direction as if they couldn't believe he hadn't picked them already, one clutched desperately at her necklace. He shut his eyes and took another deep breath. "Lila."

A chorus of sighs rushed his direction, and a lone sniffle broke the silence, but he couldn't focus on that. He needed to give Lila this hat, so this night could be over. Not only was he exhausted physically but mentally as well. He needed sleep and a few hours away from the pressure of this show. "Lila, will you accept this hat?"

"Thank you. I was so afraid you were going to send me

home." Her lips formed a small hopeful smile as she took the trinket and joined the other women.

"Ladies, if you did not receive a hat, please say your goodbyes."

Debra R placed a hand on his shoulder. "You have no idea what you're missing," she whispered to him before walking away. Stacie with an IE sobbed on his shoulder, and the other women did their best to keep a brave face on as they thanked him for the opportunity and wished him the best. Tyler saw the blanket of rejection on each one of them. It draped across their dejected shoulders and lay in their hurt-filled eyes. He knew the sting of rejection and it pained him that he was now passing on that sting to these innocent women. Even worse, he would have to do it five or six more times. Why had he ever let Nancy talk him into this?

When the five women left, he turned to the remaining fifteen knowing he should feel excited about them and the journey ahead, but he just felt zapped. He felt empty and cruel and he wanted nothing more than to crawl into his bed and pretend this day had never happened, but he couldn't. Justin had told him he had to toast with the women and let the camera catch the happy moment, so he did. He lifted his cup of apple juice - he had stipulated no alcohol for him at any time in his contract - and said his memorized toast. "To the future."

"To the future," they responded, and glasses clinked around the circle.

The words 'cut' had never sounded more amazing to Laney. Exhaustion radiated down to her core. It was nearly one am, and she was awake way past her normal bedtime. The last time she had stayed up until one in the morning was in high school when she and her partner had been cramming for a debate tournament the following day. She had barely made it through the tournament and Laney knew she'd feel the same way later today if she didn't get her eight hours of sleep.

"Ladies, please go find your suitcases. Our crew delivered them to your rooms. You may change beds but please do not change rooms. It is important we know who is in which room for safety reasons." Justin's sprayed on smile had faded and he was now all business. Probably tired himself. "Tyler, if you'll come with me, I'll take you back to your house."

Laney joined Maryanne and the rest of the crew as they followed Justin and Tyler out of the living room. Before they reached the back door, an irate voice carried down the hall. "Are you kidding me? We have to sleep four to a room?"

"Think of it like a summer camp," Laney mumbled to herself as she stepped out into the cool early morning air. She felt just a little sorry for all the women though. Summer camp had been fun for a while but a few nights of sharing a small room with other girls had a way of grating on the nerves of even the most patient person. She was certainly glad she had a room to herself.

Laney locked the door behind her and stumbled to the bedroom. She pulled back the covers and fell onto the bed. Her eyes were closed before she even hit the pillow.

12
―――

A blaring noise startled Tyler awake, and he thrashed his arm about hoping to silence the object making the noise, but he struck nothing but air.

"Sorry, it's not an alarm clock." Tyler forced his bloodshot eyes open. Justin stood over him, a smug look on his face and an alarm clock in his hand. "Or, not your normal one at least."

"What time is it?" The windows were still dark. It couldn't be past seven am.

"Five-thirty. Time to get up." How did he sound so chipper?

"Five-thirty? Dude, we just went to bed four hours ago. Why are we getting up so early?"

"That's the filming schedule for you. We have to get you in the makeup chair and you need to decide which girl you want your first solo date with. You only get one this week so use it wisely. The rest of the girls will go on two group dates with you."

Solo dates, group dates, the words swam together in Tyler's head. Three hours of sleep was simply not enough time for him to function like a normal human.

"Come on, Laney will be here in ten minutes to do your makeup. You have just enough time to get up, shower, and get dressed. She won't knock."

"All right, man. I hear you." Tyler pushed back the covers and stumbled out of the bed. As he crossed to the dresser, he was glad the room was spacious but sparsely furnished. His vision was still fuzzy from sleep, and he could picture ramming his toe into a large chest or some other piece of hulking furniture.

He opened the drawers to the dresser, rifling through them until he found his shower items and a change of clothes. At least he had his own bathroom. One of the women had told him the night before they only had two to share between all of them.

Ten minutes later, though dressed, Tyler wasn't sure he felt any more human. He pulled on clothes he hoped matched and stumbled out to the main room. Laney sat in the chair, her chin perched on her slender hand, her eyes closed. She'd probably gotten as little sleep as he did. He hated waking her as she looked so peaceful.

"Laney." He spoke her name softly as he shook her shoulder.

Her eyes popped open. "Oh my gosh, I'm so sorry. I did not mean to fall asleep."

"Don't worry, your secret's safe with me. I'm exhausted too."

She stood and stretched, then motioned for him to sit in the chair. "I sure hope the hours aren't like this every day. I'm too old to stay up like this."

"Old? You can't be more than twenty-five."

"Twenty-eight, actually, but I feel older. I haven't stayed up like this since high school." She poured the liquid makeup in the air brush machine.

"You mean it isn't always like this?" Tyler was glad he had Laney to talk to. At least conversation kept his eyes from closing.

"I don't know. This is my first time doing the show. The regular girl had to take maternity leave. But don't worry, I'm qualified," she added quickly as if afraid he might request a new girl.

"I never assumed you weren't. Are you required to do all the women's makeup as well?" The question was more to keep him awake than curiosity.

Laney chuckled as she turned on the air brush machine. "Nope, they are responsible for their own hair and makeup. They only spring for the Cowboy."

"I guess I should feel flattered?" The statement came out more like a question.

"Hah, you should. I wouldn't want to be those girls trying to cram into those tiny bathrooms."

Tyler nodded. He didn't have any sisters, but he'd dated enough women to understand they not only took over bathrooms but needed hours to get ready. He wondered if the women had gotten any sleep.

The front door opened, and Justin entered with a coffee in each hand. Tyler hoped one of them was for him. He might even rethink his judgment of Justin if it was, but alas, Justin handed the cup to Laney. She took it but appeared apprehensive. He couldn't blame her; Justin didn't give him warm fuzzies either. "Did you decide who you want to take on your solo date?"

Tyler ignored Justin's question. He couldn't think about the women when his mouth was salivating just thinking about a warm cup of coffee. "Hey, how can I get one of those?"

Justin's fake smile appeared again. "Sorry, man, crew only." Nope, he appeared irredeemable. Tyler wondered why he continued to work for the show as he certainly didn't seem to enjoy it. The money must keep him around. "There is a coffee pot in the kitchen though. Feel free to make your own if you have time."

"Right, I will. Are we done, Laney?"

"We are." She took a long sip of her coffee and smiled at him. "Go make yourself a cup. You probably have half an hour."

Half an hour. It wasn't much, but if he wanted to make it through the day, it would have to be enough. He wandered into the kitchen which was nearly the size of the women's shared kitchen and set the coffee pot percolating. A quick search through the cabinets rewarded him with not only a mug but sugar packets as well, and he poured the drink and sat down.

Justin appeared a minute later. "Okay, for one of the group dates, we've planned a horseback ride along the beach. We figure that will let you discern which women can handle being around horses. You own them, right?"

Tyler raised a brow at him. Was he serious? "Yes, I own horses. Several of them. Kinda goes with owning a ranch."

"Right, and the other group date will be a paintball adventure. You said you wanted an adventurous woman, so we hope this will let you see those willing to risk it all."

Tyler nodded. "Okay, those sound fine." He took another sip of his coffee hoping he'd be awake enough to stay on a horse and aim a gun.

"For your solo date, we're planning dinner and dancing. Have you decided who you'd like to take?"

"Uh," Tyler rubbed a hand across his forehead. It would be easier to think if he'd had more sleep. "Do all these dates happen today?"

Justin stared at him. "You've never filmed before, have you?"

"If I had would I be asking these questions?" Tyler spoke the question quietly into his mug before taking another sip, but if Justin heard him, he ignored the remark.

"The first group date will be today. The next one tomorrow, and the solo the day after."

"So, if it's only one date, why are we up so early?"

Justin rolled his eyes. "Because we must make sure we

get the coverage we need. That could take hours and the beach lighting is best early morning and evening. If we film in the morning and don't get what we want, it gives us the opportunity to film in the evening as well."

"Right." Tyler's head was spinning from the explanation. A simple answer would have sufficed, especially with his lack of sleep. "As for the solo, I'll choose Heidi." She interested him, and she seemed like someone who would enjoy dancing.

"Great. I'm going to inform the women. Be ready to go in fifteen minutes."

Fifteen minutes. He stared into his almost empty mug. Just enough time for another cup of coffee.

"Good morning ladies." Justin sounded way too chipper to Laney, especially for someone who had gotten less sleep than she had. Was he a vampire or something? Or just so used to the schedule that his body no longer fought it? She stifled a yawn and leaned against the wall as he continued.

"There will be two group dates. One today and one tomorrow. During these group dates, Tyler can decide to give you a hat early, meaning of course he plans to keep you around, or he can let you go. There will be one solo date this week before the ceremony where Tyler will cut another five of you at least."

"If all the girls cut are in one room, can we spread out

then?" one of the girls asked. Laney had dubbed this one Barbie due to her long legs and tiny waist. The other girls in the room shot her angry glances but Laney just rolled her eyes. She was used to women like this girl - the fashion world was full of them. "What?" Barbie shrugged. "I don't do three other women in my room."

"We'll talk about room arrangements after the ceremony," Justin said. "Now, we have decided on the date for today and these are the women going. Melody-" the Barbie flashed a knowing smile at the other girls, "Lila-" Melody's smile faded as she realized she wasn't on the solo date, "Cassidy, Jessica, Michelle P, Debra N. and-"

Justin paused for dramatic effect as he looked around the room. Laney wished he would just hurry up. The sooner this date got started, the sooner it could end, and she could get some sleep. "Is he always like this?" she whispered to Maryanne.

"Always, and he gets more dramatic with each episode, but he makes the best coffee." She held up her mug with a smile and then took a sip.

Laney couldn't argue with that. Though she had been apprehensive about taking the coffee when he offered it, it had turned out to be one of the best tasting blends she'd ever had.

"Kanina," Justin finished. "You seven have fifteen minutes to get ready. We roll out then."

Laney flattened herself against the wall as the women erupted in a frenzy. The seven women who were picked jumped up and began pushing their way down the hall to the bathrooms. Grunts and shouts of "Hey, watch it" carried into the living room. Some of the remaining women got up and wandered toward the kitchen. The few that stayed began a conversation about where they thought the date was taking place and who might be lucky enough to get the solo.

"What do the women not going do all day?" Laney asked Maryanne. With no television and no phone, she wondered what they had to amuse themselves.

"Most of the time, they just lie around the pool and talk. They also have a small workout room, and a closet full of games."

"Games?"

Maryanne flashed a mischievous smile. "Yep, old fashioned board games. If they get too bored, they'll pull them out. It's generally good comedy when they find the Twister game."

Laney shook her head. She'd thought this was a serious reality show, but the more she learned, the less serious it seemed. She straightened as Justin made his way over to them.

"Laney, you need to grab your supplies and head out front. You'll be riding with Tyler to the location."

"Oh, okay." Laney tried to control the fluttering in her heart at the thought of riding alone with Tyler. If only it were under different circumstances. "Guess I'll see you there," she said to Maryanne before heading out to grab her supplies.

She packed everything she thought she might need in

her travel case and then glanced in the mirror. She couldn't compare to the contestants but that was no reason not to look her best.

As she exited her bungalow, she saw Tyler leaning against a black limo, his hat pulled low on his eyes. "Hey," he said when she approached. "I guess we're riding together."

"That's what they tell me." Her voice sounded trembly in her ears, and she hoped he wouldn't notice.

He opened the door for her and stepped back. "I'm rather glad. You can punch me if I fall asleep."

Laney laughed as she climbed into the limo. "I thought that was your job, to keep me awake."

"I guess we'll have to look out for each other." He climbed in beside her and shut the door.

Laney's pulse quickened at the nearness of his body. His hand lay only inches from hers on the seat, and she was close enough to feel the heat radiating off him. Wall. She needed her wall. "So, tell me about your ranch." Maybe conversation would take her mind off the masculine scent of him that was wafting her direction.

A smile lit his features. "It's a nice place. Six hundred acres with a creek bed that runs through it. In the evenings, you can see the sunset for miles - oranges, reds, and pinks. Nothing beats a Texas sunset. Am I right?"

It had been ages since Laney had seen a Texas sunset. Even when she'd stopped home briefly, she hadn't taken the time to step outside and watch the sun set, but she did remember enjoying them in high school. She also remembered wishing Dallas Nixon would invite her out to the lookout point all the popular kids frequented Friday nights when football season was over.

"Yeah, nothing beats a Texas sunset. I bet it's even better on horseback."

"It is. There's this great spot at my ranch where the sun glistens off the creek…"

He trailed off and Laney knew he was thinking the same thing she was. She'd probably never get to see that view on his ranch because he'd be sharing it with some other woman. Laney cursed the timing of their meeting.

"It sounds lovely," Laney said and then she flew forward. Her head collided with Tyler's jaw and stars filled her vision.

"Sorry about that," the driver's voice said through the intercom. "Some kid chased a ball into the street."

"Are you hurt?" Tyler asked. His hands were on her face sending shots of heat every place his fingers touched, but Laney couldn't focus on his face. She was still seeing double.

"I think I'm okay, but man you have a hard jaw." His hands dropped from her face, and she blinked a few times until the stars receded and his two faces became one again. Was he smiling at her?

"Yeah, so I've been told."

"You've had a lot of people hit your jaw?"

His smile faded, and his eyes shifted to the side. "Not anymore."

Laney could tell there was more behind his answer, but

his face had turned to stone, and she knew better than to press the issue. Perhaps he would tell her when he was ready.

13

Tyler wasn't sure whether disappointment or relief filled him more when the limo stopped. He didn't know what he'd been thinking talking to Laney about his ranch like that. Almost like he was inviting her out when he knew he couldn't, but there was something about Laney. Something open and friendly that made him think of home and want to spill his secrets. He almost had when she'd teased him about his jaw. But she wasn't one of the contestants. She was his makeup artist, and they paid her to hang out with him. He would do well to remember that.

Perhaps that was the difference. He felt more comfortable around her because there was no pressure. He didn't have to think about giving her a hat or sending her home. He didn't have to try to imagine her fitting in his life back home, but he could. He could see her riding out with him to check the horses and then watching the sun set across the creek. He could see her sitting on his wrap-around porch, when he built one, drinking coffee with him and talking about the day. But he needed to get those thoughts out of his mind. Laney wasn't a contestant, and he had seven women waiting for him that were.

The door opened, and Tyler stepped out first holding out a hand to help Laney without thinking about it. She placed her hand in his and his fingers tingled at her touch. How long had it been since a woman had made him tingle with only a touch? Too long, but that didn't matter. He needed to stop thinking about Laney and start thinking about the other women on this date.

"Do I need a touchup?" he asked when she stood beside him.

"Nope, you look good. How do I look?" Her fingers reached for the bump on her head, but he caught her hand before she could touch it.

"You look fine. Just a little bump, but don't mess with it."

Her eyes dropped to their clasped hands before returning to his. "Okay."

"Okay," he dropped her hand - he shouldn't have been holding it in the first place, "let's go ride some horses then." Tyler led the way to the beach where the guide was waiting with ten horses. As Tyler did a mental count, he realized Laney wouldn't be riding with them today, and he wondered why they had sent her then. He hoped she wouldn't get too bored waiting for the group to return.

The women hadn't arrived yet, but he could see a limo

pulling up behind the one he and Laney had ridden in. He glanced around for Laney, but she was standing several yards away and staring out at the ocean. He wandered what she was thinking, but only briefly as the women's voices reached him.

"Horses? Is he serious?"

"Put on your game face, Jess. It's too early to go home."

"Yeah but horses are so smelly and gross."

Tyler couldn't tell which women had spoken as they approached in a group, but they obviously didn't know their voices would carry. While he wasn't sure who the second woman was, she had called the first one Jess, and the only Jess had to be Jessica who had just earned herself a ticket home. Any woman who didn't like horses would never make it on his ranch.

He put on a smile as they approached. "Welcome ladies. As you know, I live on a ranch. I spend most of my day on horseback and while my wife wouldn't have to ride with me every day, I want a woman who is comfortable riding. So, we are going for a ride down the beach."

"Awesome," Cassidy said. "I have always wanted to do this." A few other women nodded their ascent, but he noticed Jessica and Melody kept quiet. Melody must have been the other voice he heard. While he wouldn't cut her right now, he would keep his eye on her as he wasn't sure she was here for the same reason he was.

"Pick a horse, ladies, and our guide here will get you set up. Except for you, Jessica. You can go back to the house and pack your bags."

Jessica's mouth fell open and several other jaws followed suit. "What do you mean? I'm excited to ride." Her voice rose into a shrill pitch, and her eyes darted to Melody as if asking for backup.

"Actually, you're not. Any woman who thinks horses are smelly and gross won't fit in my life. I'm not sure why you're here, and I'm sure you'll make a great wife to some man someday, but it won't be me."

"But… I…" She looked around at the other women, but none were willing to back her up. She turned to Maryanne who was the closest thing to a producer in the area. "Can he do that? Just send me home?"

Maryanne looked as if she were holding back a smile. "He can indeed."

"I… but… fine," she spat the word at Tyler. "I didn't want to live on a ranch anyway. I came on this show to grow my Instagram followers, and I'm sure I'll do that." She turned to Melody, venom flowing from her eyes. "Just so you know, Melody isn't here for you either. She's here promoting her brand."

"That's not true." Melody lunged for Jessica who jumped out of the way but continued to taunt her.

"Yes, it is. Ask her about her channel."

Tyler shook his head and stepped forward. He could not believe this nonsense though he probably should have known there would be women coming on the show for their own chance at fame. "That's enough. Both of you can head back to the limo. I'm sure the driver will be glad to take you home to pack."

Melody stopped attacking Jessica to turn sugary sweet eyes on Tyler. "There's no reason to send me home too. She's making up that story because I didn't lie for her."

"That may be," Tyler said, "but I'm not a fan of your behavior just now either. I'm looking for a woman who shows grace and composure in all circumstances. So, again, you both can go now. Good luck."

Melody narrowed her eyes at him as if she were going to say more, but finally she whirled around and stalked off leaving Jessica to stumble after her.

"Well, now that the excitement is over, who's up for a ride?"

The five remaining women cheered and picked out their horses. Tyler looked around for Laney and nodded as she flashed him a small smile. He didn't need her approval but getting it felt right.

"Has that ever happened before?" Laney asked as soon as Maryanne shut the door behind them. They had dropped off the footage to Peter and Justin, stopped by the kitchen for some ice for Laney's head, and then hightailed it to Maryanne's bungalow to discuss and relax before dinner.

"No, but that was great. Peter is probably going to be angry because those two would have caused drama and drama is good for ratings, but man it was nice to see Tyler put them in their place." Maryanne collapsed onto the sofa and sighed.

"Right?" Laney sat down sideways in the chair, putting her back against one arm and throwing her legs over the other. She placed the ice bag on her head and tried not to grimace. "I worked with women like Melody a lot in New York. It was so tiring listening to them complain about everything and never being able to tell them to knock it off. You don't know how many times I practiced drawing a scar or some hideous birthmark on their head shots."

Maryanne's eyes widened. "You did no such thing."

"Okay, I didn't," Laney said with a roll of her eyes. "I never even saw their headshots, but I thought about it."

"Her face reminded me of Mr. Cuthbert's in high school. Remember that day when you showed him the petition?"

Laney's free hand flew to her mouth as the memory came back to her. "He was so mad. I think he would have kept me from graduating if he could have found a way." Laney had never been a fan of injustice and she fought hard for things she considered unfair. When the principal had shut down their new stage her senior year because someone graffitied the 'Exit' sign, Laney had typed up a petition and gathered signatures from the students. Then she had taken the petition to the district office. The woman in charge there had sent her back to Mr. Cuthbert, but she must have called and said something to him because when Laney, Maryanne, and Jennifer, their other friend, had arrived, he had been fuming.

"What was it he said?" Maryanne asked. Her face scrunched in thought, but Laney didn't have to try to remember. His words were forever imprinted on her mind.

"You went above my head," she started. Maryanne's eyes snapped open and she finished the statement with Laney, "to a woman?"

"He was such a jerk," Maryanne said shaking her head.

"Yeah, but he taught me strength and the importance of standing up for what you believe in. I think I'd kind of forgotten that over the last few years. Thank you for reminding me." Laney thought back over the months she had worked for Madame Bonavich and realized she was just as bad as Mr. Cuthbert had been if not worse, and yet Laney had taken her abuse day after day. How had she let the opinion of one boy who had never noticed her and who she'd probably never see again influence her life so profoundly?

"I'm really glad we reconnected," Maryanne said. "I didn't think I missed any of you, but now that you're here, I realize I do. I've missed you and the rest of the group. Maybe when this show is over we should try to get the gang together."

Laney was just about to agree when a knock sounded at the door. She looked to Maryanne who shrugged but crossed to the door and opened it. "Maryanne, have you seen Laney? I need to talk to her."

Peter's voice sounded almost frantic and Laney stood as Maryanne stepped back. His eyes took in Laney and he hurried over to her. "Oh good, you're here. I need to talk to you. I know we were only going to have you do Tyler's makeup, but I just watched the footage from today, and the women need some help. Can you please do their makeup as well for the rest of the show?"

Laney bit her lip as she thought about what to say. The logical part of her wanted to say yes, of course she could. That was her job after all, but the emotional part of her wasn't sure she could handle making the women even more beautiful. Even though she knew he was off limits and she had no idea if he was even interested in her, there was this crazy part of her that felt like she was competing for Tyler too and making the contestants even more beautiful would just push her farther down the ladder.

In the end, her logical side won out and she nodded. "Sure, Peter, I'd be happy to. Just let me know when and remember I need ten to fifteen minutes per woman plus Tyler."

"Great, I'll add it to the production schedule. We'll make sure we have enough time before the next date. Thank you, Laney, you are a lifesaver."

As he hurried out of the room, Laney sank back down in the chair. What had she just agreed to?

14

Laney took a deep breath and opened the door to the women's house. She couldn't believe she had agreed to do this, but what was she supposed to say? "I can't do the women's makeup because I'm attracted to Tyler?" Yeah that would have gone over well. They would probably have fired her on the spot. There had been nothing in the contract about falling for the Cowboy, but Laney also noted that all the other women on the crew wore a wedding ring already. Maybe this was why.

"Ah, there you are." Justin stood just inside the door looking like his usual plastic self. Laney wondered if he did his own makeup or if that was his natural look. "I had Maryanne gather the women together. I was just about to tell them about the date tonight. Come with me."

Laney followed Justin into the living room where the women sat like an attentive audience. It was weird how they focused completely on Justin, but Laney assumed it was because this was the highlight of their day. With no television, phone, or outside communication, the women must get bored the rest of the day. Most of the live footage she'd watched with Maryanne had been boring. The girls making a sandwich, the girls getting a drink, the girls sitting by the pool. Laney wondered why they bothered filming it at all.

"Tonight's date will be an adventure, and I will tell you who is going in just a moment, but you might wonder why Laney is here." A few of the girls nodded and looked her direction, but most kept their focus on Justin. "Laney is Tyler's makeup artist. We don't normally have her do the contestants too, but we noticed on the last take that some of the women's makeup was less than desirable on HD, so Laney is here to make sure you look your best. Is that clear?"

The girls nodded, and Justin continued. "Great, so going on tonight's date is Michelle C, Erica, Bristol, Peyton, Rachel, Jenna, and Jade. Heidi, congratulations, you have the first solo date tomorrow night." Heidi beamed, and the other girls shot her envious looks. "So, if I called your name, please stay, and if I didn't, please vacate the room to give Laney room to work."

The six women not called stood and left the room, and Laney glanced at the remaining seven. "Okay, let's start with you." She pointed to the pretty brunette who sat in the single chair.

"I'm Erica," the girl said scooting toward the edge of the chair. "So, what's it like doing Tyler's makeup?"

"Uh," Laney held up her foundation to try to match Erica's complexion. "It's fine. Just like doing anyone else's I guess."

"Is his face soft?"

"Uh." His jaw certainly wasn't as the bump still visible on her forehead proclaimed, but she hadn't touched his face, at least not in the way this girl meant.

"Does he talk about us?"

"Yeah, has he said who he likes best?"

The girls fired questions at Laney one after the other. They were like rabid fans at a concert. Laney answered as vaguely as possible not wanting to share the piece of Tyler she had access to that the women didn't.

"He doesn't really talk about it much."

When it became clear Laney couldn't or wouldn't answer any more of their questions, the women ignored her and chatted with each other. Their conversations subtly shifted into catty observations of the women not in the room.

"I can't understand why he chose Heidi for his solo date," one girl said.

"Yeah, what does he see in her?"

Laney bit her lip to keep from interjecting into the conversation. She wasn't supposed to get involved but listening to women disparage each other wasn't something she enjoyed. Relief flooded her veins when she finished the last woman's make up. She packed up her supplies and headed out to Tyler's room.

∽

Tyler smiled as Laney entered his room, but his smile changed to a look of concern at her pinched expression. "What's the matter?"

"Oh nothing. I was just asked to do the women's makeup as well, and I forgot how catty women can be when they get together." She pulled out the makeup and set it on the table.

"Catty? What do you mean?"

Laney rolled her eyes. "Just talking about the women who had gone on the previous date and poor Heidi who you chose for the solo." Laney's eyes widened, and she clasped her hand over her mouth. "Oh my gosh, I'm so sorry. I'm not supposed to talk about the women in front of you. Please don't tell anyone what I said."

"Hey," he put his hand on her arm - she looked so vulnerable at this moment, and his heart ached with her, "your secret is safe with me. Why aren't you supposed to talk about the women?"

Her eyes dropped to his hand, and her teeth bit down on her bottom lip. "I guess they think I might influence your decision. As if you cared about my opinion."

She turned away, and his hand fell away from her arm, but he wasn't letting her off that easily. He grabbed her hand and turned her back to him. "I do care about your opinion." She looked down at their hands and then back up at him. "I'm not sure why I do except that you're the person I feel closest to here."

"I am?" Her voice was quiet. Breathy.

"Yeah, I mean I'm kind of shut up in here except for when you come over and when I go on the dates, and while the women seem nice, I don't get to talk to them the way you and I do. Besides, we're kindred spirits both being from Texas. You know what they say. You can take the girl out of Texas, but you can't take Texas out of the girl."

"I... um," she pulled her hand out from his grasp. "I should do your makeup." Her eyes shifted from his and to the table where she rearranged the items she had just placed.

Right. What had he been thinking? Laney worked for the show, and he had probably just made her uncomfortable. Besides, even if she had been a contestant, she was a city girl, and he knew how well those worked out. He needed to be professional from now on with her. Still, he wanted to know more about her.

"So, what made you become a makeup artist?" It seemed like an innocent question, but he saw Laney's shoulders tense as she poured the foundation into the air brush machine.

"It's a rather stupid reason," she said with a forced laugh. "I wanted to learn makeup, so I wouldn't be invisible anymore."

"Invisible? You are anything but invisible."

"Ha. That's nice of you to say, but I've always been the girl who is everyone's *friend*." The way she emphasized the word friend let him know that men overlooked her. For some reason, they didn't see her as dating material, and he wondered why. True, he didn't know her well, but she was funny and sweet and pretty and… He needed to stop that train of thought right now. She was not the woman for him.

He wanted to say something to put a smile back on her face, but appropriate words failed him, and before any sprang to mind, she was already spraying his face and packing up.

"All done," she said, her eyes avoiding his gaze, "have fun tonight."

"Thanks, I'll try." But he wondered if he'd be able to focus on anything other than Laney's words. "Wait, you're not going?"

She shrugged. "It's paintball. The point is to get dirty, so they said they don't need me there to pretty you all up."

"Right, well I guess I'll see you tomorrow?"

"I'll be here." She flashed a small smile before exiting his room, and Tyler sank down into the chair. He needed to focus on tonight's date and get Laney's face out of his mind, but that was easier said than done.

A knock sounded, and his door opened. "You ready?" Justin asked.

"Yep, let's do this." Tyler put on his best smile and followed Justin out of his room. He would get through tonight and re-evaluate his feelings. Surely, he was just feeling closer to Laney because he spent the most time with her. Once he had his solo date, things were sure to change. At least he hoped they did.

Laney glanced up from her Bible as her bungalow door swung open, and Maryanne blew in, shutting the door behind her.

"You are never going to believe what happened." She plopped down next to Laney on the couch and folded one leg underneath her. "I can't believe you weren't there, but I'll try to do it justice. Oh, man, they are going to be so mad. Heads are probably spinning right now."

Laney chuckled at the whirlwind that was her friend and closed her Bible. She wouldn't be able to focus now. "Okay, it sounds intriguing, but you're going to have to slow down and start at the beginning because I am so lost right now."

"It's Tyler, he's like no cowboy we've ever had."

Laney wanted to ask how he was different, but Maryanne had already moved on.

"So, they went paintballing, right? But, Bristol threw a fit over having to wear the protective gear. Said it wasn't flattering and would ruin her hair."

"And he sent her home?" Laney offered.

Maryanne threw her hands up in the air. "He sent her home. The men don't usually send women home on the dates. They usually wait for the ceremony, so we can *have* a ceremony. If he keeps this up, we may not have enough women to do a ceremony. I'm sure Peter and Justin are freaking out right now about what to do about him."

"Well, he obviously knows what he wants or what he

doesn't want anyway." Laney's admiration for Tyler grew even more. He didn't seem to want to play their game and that made him different. And appealing. But she couldn't act on those feelings. Wouldn't act on those feelings. He might seem different now, but deep down he was probably like all the other men Laney had known in her life. The kind who said they wanted one thing but really wanted another.

15

"Well, you've caused quite the stir," Laney said when Tyler opened the door. He looked incredible in his jeans and plaid shirt and Laney had to force her eyes to stay on his face rather than travel down his body.

"Whatever do you mean?" His words might have been curious, but his smile was sly as he stepped back and allowed her entrance. He knew exactly what she meant.

"I mean I just spent the last three hours with the rest of the crew brainstorming how to save this show if you keep sending all the women home early."

"Yeah, and what did they decide?"

Was he smiling? He was. Like a Cheshire cat. He was enjoying this. "Are you doing this on purpose?"

"On purpose?" A teasing glint appeared in his eyes. "I suppose it depends on what you mean by on purpose. Am I sending women home I don't see a future with on purpose?

Yes, I am, but if you mean am I trying to ruin the show on purpose? No, I'm not. I came on this show for two reasons. Well, three if you count Nancy."

"Nancy? Who's Nancy?" Did he have a woman at home?

"Nancy is my best friend's wife. Remember, I told you she convinced me to come on the show."

Relief flooded Laney. Oh geez, relief? She needed to get a hold on her emotions. She wasn't competing for him. "Right, I do remember you saying that. So, what are the other two reasons?" Laney walked past him to seem uninterested though she was hanging on his every word. She put her makeup case down and opened the lid. Look busy. She needed to look busy.

"One reason is the money. I don't know if they pay the women, but they pay me, and as much as I don't like doing things for the money, I need it to keep my ranch going."

Something in the sincerity of his voice made Laney turn back to look at him. "Your ranch means a lot to you, doesn't it?"

"It does. I grew up on a ranch and always knew it was what I wanted to do."

"And what about the last reason?" Laney's breath caught in her throat as she asked the question. She hoped he was looking for love and yet she didn't. If he was, it meant he probably wasn't just playing some game like Maryanne said they often did, but it also meant that he might find it with someone other than herself. If he wasn't, then he wasn't the man she thought he was. Neither answer really held a win for Laney.

He took a step toward her, and Laney felt electricity crackle in the air. "I hoped perhaps I might find love. Maybe that's silly with this being a reality show and not ordinary circumstances, but I live in a small town. Not a lot of fish in that sea. I guess I hoped I might meet someone special here."

"And have you?"

His eyes tore through hers like he was reading every inch of her soul. Laney wanted to close the book. She couldn't be vulnerable for him, but her feet were glued to the floor, her body frozen in place.

"I can't say I've found love, but I've certainly found something I'd like to explore more." His gaze felt like a caress on her face sending a streak of fire from her cheek all the way down to the floor. He liked her? But he couldn't like her. She wasn't a contestant. It would never work, but she couldn't deny she felt something for him any longer.

"Tyler, I..." She didn't get to finish the sentence as the door opened then and Justin's voice carried into the room.

"Laney, I need you to -" Even though they hadn't been touching when the door opened, Laney knew they looked guilty, and she could tell from Justin's face that he had seen enough to suspect something, but oddly he said nothing just finished his sentence, "do Heidi's makeup in twenty minutes."

Laney didn't like the look in his eyes. They gleamed wickedly like an older brother who had just obtained dirt he could use to frame his younger sibling. "Sure, I'll be there in a bit. I need to finish with Tyler."

When the door closed behind Justin, Laney spoke first. "We better get started." Though the look wasn't forgotten, she didn't have time to deal with it or it's ramifications right now.

Tyler wanted to discuss the moment. He had wanted to kiss Laney. He wanted to tell her he wished she was a contestant, but the second Justin left, she had become all business again. He didn't blame her; he'd seen the spark in Justin's eyes as he knew she had. Tyler was wary of Justin at the best of times, but he was even more wary now having no idea what Justin might do with what he had seen. Would he revoke Tyler's contract? Fire Laney? Though he needed the money, Tyler wouldn't be too hurt if they revoked his contract. Then he could pursue Laney himself.

He waited patiently as she changed his tie and applied his makeup hoping the right words would come into his head, but he kept coming up blank. "Laney," he began when she finished and began packing her supplies, "we need to talk about-"

"We will," she said cutting him off. Her eyes did not meet his though. "Just not right now. You have your solo date to focus on and I have to go do her makeup." With that, she closed her case and walked out of his room.

Tyler sighed and ran a hand through his hair. Maybe

he should just talk to Justin, tell him he felt something for Laney, more than he did for the contestants. He might lose the money, but he thought he might gain something even greater.

Tonight, he decided. He would find Justin after his date with Heidi and tell him everything. Laney had said they were trying to figure out what to do with the show. Maybe this would help them. Maybe it wasn't too late to get another cowboy and new women in.

Pulling his shoulder back, he left the room. Tonight, he would get to ride with Heidi, so he might as well be waiting by the limo when she arrived.

"You look beautiful," he said fifteen minutes later when she emerged from the main house in a stunning green dress. Laney had done a wonderful job on her makeup somehow drawing more attention to her already arresting green eyes. Her red hair lay piled on her head, but a few curly tendrils escaped and coiled by her ears. It surprised him to feel his breath catch a little. How could he feel attracted to Heidi and Laney at the same time? They were completely different people.

"Thank you. You look handsome as well."

He opened the limo door for her. "Shall we?"

"We shall." She climbed in first scooting over to leave him room. After shutting the door, he settled in beside her.

"How is the experience going for you?" he asked. It was a rather dumb and mundane question, but this was one of the first times he had gotten to chat with her without the other women or even the camera around.

"It's definitely an experience." She said the words in a way that left him wondering if that was good or bad. "I grew up in a large family so sharing the house hasn't been so bad, but that many women together…" She shook her head, and he understood her meaning.

"I wondered about that. What do you do for entertainment?" They didn't let him see the women except for the dates and the ceremony night, and he wondered if they were often as bored as he was.

"I try to read. They let me keep my Bible though they took all the rest of my books."

"You're a believer then?" He wasn't keeping a mental tally of Heidi's qualities, but had he been, she would have gained another check.

"Of course. God is important to me. It's getting a lot harder to teach in the public schools where I am now. I mean they haven't let God in for years, but now… well, let's just say they allow in almost everything except God, and I teach preschool. I can't even imagine how much harder it is for high school teachers."

Tyler couldn't imagine either. He rarely watched the news because it seemed like every time he turned it on, he could see how the rest of the world was moving farther away from God. His community was small and most of them attended church, so he felt a little sheltered from the war waging outside.

He was almost disappointed when the limo pulled to a stop in front of a breathtaking restaurant that overlooked an inlet. They still had the rest of the evening, but once they got inside, there would be the camera and other people watching. Tyler knew it wouldn't quite be the same.

He was tempted to hold her hand as they walked up the sidewalk, but the moment with Laney was still too fresh in his mind. He glanced around for the camera. Shouldn't Maryanne and Laney be here already? Maybe they had told Laney she could skip this one, but there was no way they wouldn't film this date.

A host dressed in black slacks and a white shirt opened the main door for them as they approached. "Mr. Hall," he said with a nod, "if you'll follow me. We have your table all set up."

Ah, so perhaps they had arrived first and would be waiting for them. The lights in the restaurant were dim creating a romantic atmosphere, and Tyler could feel his connection with Heidi growing. They followed the host past the other patrons to a private room at the back. An elegant table for two had been set up with candles adding a little more light to the area. The camera was up, and the lights were on, but there was no sign of Maryanne or Laney. Had they decided to just let the camera roll? Perhaps the producers had thought they would be a distraction, and they weren't wrong. Even though he was attracted to Heidi, the moment with Laney earlier still played in his mind.

"This is lovely," Heidi said placing a hand on his arm.

He forced his attention back to her. "Yes, it is." Focus. He needed to focus on her. He owed her that. He owed himself that. With a smile, he pulled out her chair for her and pushed it in after she sat down. A basket of bread and butter sat in the middle of the table, but he noticed she took none. Simply folded her hands in her lap.

"The chef has prepared a special menu for you tonight. I'll leave this with you, and the chef will be out soon to take your order himself," the host said as he handed them a single sheet of cardstock-like paper.

Tyler scanned the paper surprised to only see six options on it. The appetizers consisted of Duck Pâté en Croûte or Escargots a la Bourguignonne. He wasn't exactly sure what Duck Pâté en Croûte was, but he knew the other was snails and he had no desire for those. Some steak dish and what he thought was a fish dish were the only entree choices and then there were two for dessert as well. Tyler had never understood the draw of fancy restaurants like these; he preferred places where he could not only pronounce what he was ordering but knew that it would fill him up.

"This so reminds me of Paris. I'm so glad they chose a French restaurant."

"You've been to Paris?" Tyler found that surprising on a teacher's salary. He knew they didn't make as much as people generally assumed as his mother had been a teacher before she retired. They'd never had the money for exotic vacations even with both his parents earning an income.

"Oh yeah, I go every year. France and Italy. My parents own a vineyard in Washington state, and we like to travel around tasting wines from different wineries to see what maybe we should add."

A cold stone settled in Tyler's stomach. "So, your family must drink a lot."

Heidi giggled. "Well, we don't get drunk but yeah wine is served at every meal. Why is that a problem? You're not against drinking, are you?"

"Morally, no, but I'm a recovering alcoholic. I can't be around alcohol at every meal."

"Oh." Heidi's voice fell flat, and Tyler knew what she was thinking. This was a deal breaker. Wine was important to her family, and he would never ask her to give it up, but there was no way he would be able to be around it that often. While he could opt out of the family vacations or dinners, he knew that would cause resentment in the future and tear them apart. Even their shared faith probably wasn't enough to overcome these obstacles.

"Yeah, but hey that doesn't mean we can't enjoy a nice dinner, right? Give you a reminder of France before you go?"

"You'd stay even though you know we can't work?" Heidi looked at him as if he'd just grown a third eye. He must have gotten a reputation among the women sending them home as often as he did.

Tyler shrugged. "We have to eat, right?" He picked up his water glass and took a drink.

"That we do. You know, I wouldn't have to drink wine with every meal. We could abstain together, and maybe we could find other things to see on the vacations."

He appreciated that she was offering a compromise, but he didn't think she would really be happy if she followed through with it. "Do you think you'd be okay with that? I mean, it would mean breaking from the family tradition."

Her teeth nibbled on her bottom lip. "I'd like to think I could try."

"That's sweet, Heidi, but this isn't something that's going to go away for me. I don't drink when I go out, I don't keep liquor in my house, and I avoid situations where a lot of people are drinking. It's just too tempting."

Heidi picked up a piece of bread and turned it in her hands. "I guess you're right. I'm just disappointed because I think we might have been good together. Minus this fact, of course."

"God has a plan for everything, and I have no doubt his hand is in this. Maybe your perfect man will see you on this show and come into your life."

Heidi chuckled at that but picked up her water glass. "I'll toast to that and to new friends."

With a smile, Tyler raised his glass and clinked it against hers, but now that he knew Heidi wasn't the woman for him, his mind went back to the other woman who seemed to continually pop up there. He had just told Heidi he believed God was in control, but then how did he explain his feelings for Laney?

16

*L*aney glanced up as the kitchen door opened and froze. She had come in here to do her devotional and drown her feelings in a bowl of ice cream, but she had not expected to run into Tyler.

"Oh, Tyler, what are you doing here?" She didn't think they would approve of her being in the room with him if she wasn't doing his makeup. That probably went against her contract.

"I was looking for some of that." He pointed to her carton of ice cream. "You mind if I share?"

The correct answer was neither yes nor no, but leaving the room, especially after their interaction earlier, but her body refused to move. "Um, I guess not."

He grabbed a spoon from the drawer and sat across from her. "What are you reading?"

"I was doing my devotional. I'm in the book of Luke."

"You're a believer too?"

There was surprise but not condescension in his voice. Still, she answered slowly unsure of where this conversation was going. "I am." He nodded but said nothing as he scooped up a bite of ice cream. She decided to pry a little. "Did the date not go well?" She tried to keep her focus on the bowl, but her eyes glanced up at him.

"It started out well. I found out Heidi was a believer too." A feeling of dread settled in Laney's stomach. Was he about to tell her he'd decided Heidi was the one for him? "Unfortunately, it turns out her family also owns a winery and wine is an integral part of their family."

"And that's a bad thing because?"

Tyler put down his spoon and stared at her. "Do you drink?"

The question caught her off guard, and Laney blinked a few times as she processed it. "I'm not much of a drinker. I watched my dad get drunk on New Year's Eve once and he acted so stupid. While I can't say I never drink, it's certainly something I could live without. Why do you ask?"

"Because I'm a recovering alcoholic," the look he shot her was almost a challenge, "and I can't be with a woman who drinks."

A light flicked on as a piece of the puzzle clicked into place. "Is that you meant about your jaw? Did you get in fights when you were drinking?"

He ran a hand across his chin and dropped his gaze. "I did. It's not something I'm proud of, but it's something I've worked hard to overcome. So, I can't date a woman who surrounds herself with alcohol."

"Well, that is understandable." Why was he telling her this? "I'm sorry things with Heidi didn't work out."

He took another bite as he continued to stare at her. "Are you?"

The question flustered Laney. What was she supposed to say to that? "I mean, yeah, that's why you came on the show, right? To find a partner?"

"And what if I find someone I think would make a great partner, but she isn't a contestant?"

Laney's breath caught in her throat. Was he talking about her? He had to be. There was no other explanation. She wanted to tell him that he should tell her, that he should leave the show and pursue her, but then she thought of the ramifications. He would lose his contract and the money he needed for his ranch. So, she didn't tell him those things. Instead, she said words she never expected to come out of her mouth. "I think you should focus on finding a partner among the contestants."

He opened his mouth as if to protest, but Laney didn't let him. "I wish you luck, and I guess I'll see you tomorrow before the ceremony." She grabbed her Bible and hurried from the room. Tears were already starting to blur her vision, and she didn't want Tyler seeing them.

Tyler tried to focus on what Lila was saying, but his mind refused to forget the night before with Laney. She felt something for him. He was sure she did, but why hadn't she said so. He had given her the perfect opening, and she hadn't taken it. Then she had barely spoken to him today while doing his makeup. Had he read her wrong? Maybe she wasn't single, just friendly? But he didn't think so.

"You're a lot nicer than I expected. People told me horror stories about men from Texas - how they dominated their women and carried guns everywhere, but you don't seem like that at all." She giggled and placed a hand on his arm.

Her words grabbed his attention, and for a moment Laney flew from his mind. "What? I mean, I have guns, but they're to protect my cattle from coyotes and other wild animals, and I have no desire to dominate a woman. I want a partner. Who told you such nonsense?" He was overreacting, and he knew it, but he was upset. Why was he having to feign interest in a woman like this when the woman he wanted to be talking to was back in her bungalow?

Lila bit her lip and removed her hand as if worried she had upset him. "Oh, that makes so much more sense. Perhaps they were just messing with me. I am a little gullible."

"Well, I'm glad I could clarify for you." Tyler didn't care at all, but he knew his frustration had little to do with Lila's misconceptions and more about his issue with Laney.

"I'm glad you could too. I was actually terrified to go to your ranch."

"Why?" Tyler could only imagine what her friends must have told her about ranchers.

Pink flamed across her cheeks and the dropped her eyes to her hands. "I thought you would make us shoot an animal and cook it for dinner."

At this Tyler laughed out loud. "I don't hunt my food. I raise cattle to sell, and while I have chickens, it's for their eggs and not their meat. My food I buy at the grocery store like you do."

She bit her lip and tucked a strand of hair behind her ear. "I feel a little silly, but I'd never been to Texas and my friends swore they had. Of course I realized not all of Texas was like that, but when I heard you were from a small town, I guess I just assumed. That's awful, I shouldn't assume."

She looked so dejected that Tyler reached over and squeezed her hand. "It's okay. We all do it sometimes. I'm just glad you get to go back with the truth."

"Me too." She stared up at him with big doe eyes that almost made him want to give her a second chance, but he was tired of doing the same thing over and over again. In fact, wasn't that the definition of insanity? Doing the same things again and expecting a different outcome? He had dated too many women who he connected with momentarily but wanted different things out of life, so even though Lila was beautiful and sweet, he knew a relationship with her would never last. And that was what he wanted. A relationship. That lasted. The only problem was that he wanted a relationship with Laney and she seemed unable or unwilling to give it a shot with him. He needed to know why, and he needed to do it before the ceremony.

17

Laney looked from Peter to Justin with wide eyes. "You can't be serious." The ceremony was scheduled to start any minute.

"We're very serious." Peter leaned back in the large leather chair and crossed one leg over the other. "You were in the meeting the other day. We need to do something drastic especially after he sent Heidi home. She was the focus group's favorite after the first two episodes. We need a favorite or there's nothing for the fans to watch."

"And you two obviously have a connection," Justin spoke up. He looked almost giddy, and Laney wanted to slap his plastic smile off his face.

"Look what you saw the other day-"

"Was an attraction," he finished for her, "and I've been watching him since. Even if he had felt something for Heidi, what he feels for you is stronger."

Laney's emotions careened around like a roller coaster.

They wanted her to be a contestant. On one hand, her heart was jumping up and down at the opportunity. This meant the chance to date Tyler to see if their connection was real. But she'd have to be a contestant. She'd have to be on television. And she'd have to deal with the other women. Laney sucked in her breath. "What about the other women? They'll hate me. They know I've spent more time with Tyler. Why would they even stay?"

Peter folded his hands and leaned forward placing his elbows on the table. She hated how calm he appeared as if this were the most natural solution in the world. "We've thought about that too. The other girls will be jealous, yes, but those feelings will add some conflict to the show. It was lacking after he sent the first two women away. Plus, we have come up with an incentive for them to stay. They'll have the option to leave when it's announced you are joining, but for those who stay, we're going to offer a guaranteed spot on our tropical spin-off series Match Made in Maui that will be kicking off soon."

Laney wasn't sure how many women left were on the show just for the fame, but she could imagine there were at least a few. An incentive of more face time might be enough to keep them around. "And what about me? Is there a bonus for me?"

"You mean beyond the bonus of getting to date a man you are clearly attracted to?" Justin eyebrow arched on his forehead. It didn't even create a wrinkle. He must use Botox. Nobody's face was that wrinkle free.

She fixed an even stare on him. "Yes, I mean beyond

that. As much as I would like to date Tyler, you are asking me to walk into a hostile situation and have our relationship unfold on national television. That's not always the best foundation for a lasting relationship, so yeah I want to know what's in it for me beyond that."

"A job with us until Talia returns from maternity leave." Her head whipped back to Peter. "And a recommendation from us after that. This is California, Laney, there are a lot of studios and modeling agencies around here that could use your talent."

Laney bit her lip. While it wasn't a guaranteed job offer, it was as close to one as she could get and that meant security and money. Money, especially for someone who had recently gotten fired and had moved all her belongings back to Texas, was certainly appealing. "What about Tyler? Does he know about this?"

Justin's lips pulled back into that plastic smile. "This was Tyler's idea. He came in here just an hour ago to tell us that he wanted to pursue you. He offered to walk off the show and void his contract."

Laney stared at the men. Tyler had offered to forfeit the money he needed for his ranch for her?

"Peter and I happen to think this is a better idea. Everyone wins."

Laney wasn't sure about that. The deal might have a perk for everyone involved, but she could also see about a dozen ways it could go incredibly wrong. Still, a chance with Tyler and the money was quite appealing. "Can I have an hour to pray about it?"

Justin chuckled and leaned back. "You two really are perfect for each other."

"What do you mean?" Laney asked.

"I mean that's exactly what he said when I laid out the option for him."

Laney's heart leapt in her chest, but she mashed her lips together to keep from smiling. She'd guessed he was a believer after their conversation the previous night, but she was glad for the confirmation. Perhaps that explained some of their chemistry. A love for the Lord combined with common roots of both being from Texas made their connection make sense. "Good, then I'll take that as a yes. I'll pray about it and let you know my decision in an hour." She turned to Peter, "I assume I'll have to move out of the bungalow and into the house?"

"Those are the rules."

"And what about the makeup? Who will do it now?"

"We've already got calls in for that," Peter said. "You just let us know your decision and we'll handle the rest. We will continue to pay you through the end of the show as well."

Laney nodded and pushed back her chair. "I'll let you know soon." She tried to focus her emotions as she walked back to her bungalow. This was a big decision and one that could change her life.

Tyler couldn't believe he was facing yet another

ceremony. He had thought offering to leave the show would keep him from this, but Peter and Justin had presented another option. He didn't know if Laney would take it, but the fact that he was still in the deliberation room gave him hope she would.

What if she had left? He'd agreed to stay only if she did, so the fact that Justin hadn't released him gave him hope, but then why hadn't the ceremony started yet? Maybe Justin was telling the women. If they all agreed to stay, Tyler would have to send two home tonight. He took the moment to go over them in his head.

During the first group date, Cassidy had stood out. She hadn't vied for his attention like some of the other women and she'd been comfortable on the back of the horse. At lunch, she'd ordered a burger and not a salad like most of the other women further endearing herself to him. He didn't mind a woman ordering a salad if that's what she wanted, but he was tired of women ordering salads to lose weight.

Michelle C. had stolen his focus on the second group date. She was fearless, not caring if she got hit or dirty. Her moves had put the other women to shame. He'd had a chance to talk with Erica and Peyton at dinner and they were both spunky and fun, but the rest of the women he hadn't had much time with nor had they stolen his focus. How would he choose the two women to send home?

"Sorry I'm late," Justin said as he opened Tyler's door. "Are you ready for the ceremony?"

"I'm assuming since there is one that Laney agreed to become a contestant?"

Justin shrugged but said nothing. Tyler supposed he would find out shortly. He followed Justin into the living room where the eleven women stood. Confusion covered all their faces as well. Justin continued past them to the table at the front of the room where ten little hats sat.

"Welcome ladies and Tyler. Now, I'm sure you're all wondering why the ceremony is so late tonight." A few of the women nodded and looked around at their fellow competitors. "Well, since Tyler is so clear on what he doesn't want, we've eliminated more women than we usually do by now. We're afraid if he keeps this up, we might not have enough episodes to fill the season, so we decided to make it a little more interesting. We are bringing in someone Tyler has appeared to be attracted to-"

"What? That's not fair," Rachel spoke up. "We've been competing all week. It isn't right to bring someone new in." The other girls nodded in agreement.

"I understand how you ladies feel but remember we're all here to try to find Tyler a wife. However, we thought about you ladies when we made this decision." He picked up a hat. "Should you decide to leave and not accept Tyler's hat, that is understandable. However, should you decide to stay, you should know that this new girl will not be allowed one of the solo dates before we go to Tyler's ranch, Tyler won't be able to send women home during a date from here on out, and there is a special surprise for those of you who decide to stay. We've left you the details in your room, but you can't read it until you accept the hat."

The girls looked to Tyler, but he simply shrugged. This was news to him, and he wasn't sure he liked some of the requirements they had added, but if it meant Laney was staying, he would go along with it.

"Do we at least get to know who the woman is first?" Kanina asked.

"Afraid not. The woman will arrive after the ceremony, so you will find out tonight. Those of you watching at home will have to wait for next week, I'm afraid." Justin's smile looked anything but apologetic as he stared out at the women and the camera. "Shall we get started?" The women looked at each other, but as none walked out, Tyler was fairly certain that was their way of agreeing. "Fantastic. I'll just take this for the mystery woman," Justin indicated the hat in his hand, "and Tyler can give out the rest. Looks like only two of you will be going home tonight. Tyler?"

Tyler nodded though he wasn't sure he was ready. He picked up the first hat and glanced around the room. The women smiled at him with nervous anticipatory smiles, but one face was missing. Laney was not in attendance, and Tyler wasn't sure if that made the process easier or harder. "Cassidy."

She smiled and stepped forward accepting his hat and stepping to the side.

"Michelle C." The process continued until he had just one hat left. He looked at the three remaining women. Lila had her eyes closed and her lips moved slightly as if silently praying, Jade stared down at her feet, but Debra N stared directly at him. This was the part he hated the most. Though he wasn't sure he could see a future with any of these women, sending them home felt like rejecting them personally, and he'd had enough of that in his life to know it affected them. "Jade."

As she smiled and stepped forward, he saw Lila cover her face with her hands. He had made her cry, and he hated himself for it.

"Lila, Debra, please take a moment and say your goodbyes."

Lila walked over to him, her makeup already streaking down her cheeks from her tears. "I thought we had a connection. We just needed more time. Was this about earlier? I'm really sorry."

Tyler looked to Justin for help, but the man seemed content to watch the display. "I'm sorry, Lila. You will find your perfect man someday." His empty words did little to console her, but she nodded and shuffled away.

Debra was a little more composed. She hugged him lightly and wished him luck before exiting the room.

Though he knew he had to toast and celebrate with the women, Tyler wanted nothing more than to disappear to his room or go find Laney. Justin had said she would be joining, so, where was she?

Laney took a bite of her ice cream and stared down at her Bible. She'd have to go join the other women shortly, but she wanted to enjoy her last meal in the quiet. She still had no idea of what would happen once she was in the house. Maybe the women would be civil, but Laney wasn't counting on it.

The kitchen door opened, and she smiled up at Maryanne. "The ceremony over then?"

"Yep, whenever you're ready. Are you sure you want to do this? I mean I know you like him; I could tell the first day, but what if he turns out to be-" she bit her lip to keep from saying the words.

"Another Dallas Nixon?"

"I wasn't going to say it."

"He's no Dallas, Maryanne. I had a crush on Dallas for four years and he never gave me the time of day. Tyler has already shown more interest than that."

"I know, but what if he changes when you're a contestant?"

"I don't see that happening. Tyler seems like the real deal. He offered to walk off the show for me. To be honest, I'm much more worried about Justin."

Maryanne's face scrunched in confusion. "Why Justin?"

Laney shook her head. "I don't know. He had this look on his face when he suggested this. I have this feeling he's going to try to sabotage it somehow. I just don't know how."

"Justin's harmless. He's vain and annoying but

harmless. If you trust Tyler, then I'm sure it will be fine. Speaking of which, are you ready?"

Laney nodded and placed her bowl in the sink. Then she closed her Bible and tucked it in her bag before following Maryanne out of the kitchen and into the main house. She could hear the hum of conversation as they approached the living room, and Laney took a deep breath. *Here goes nothing.*

The conversations stopped as Laney and Maryanne entered the room. "Ladies meet your number ten." Maryanne squeezed her arm before turning and leaving the room.

Laney smiled out at the women, but a sea of severe faces stared back at her.

"She's the number ten? The bonus better be worth it," one woman said before exiting the room.

Laney sought Tyler's eyes across the room. The other women surrounded him, but he smiled at her and flashed a wink. Laney smiled back. It wasn't much, but that wink would have to be enough for now.

18
---

*L*aney was looking forward to the date even if it would be a group date. She'd been in the main house for nearly a week and most of the girls avoided her or gave her the cold shoulder - not that she blamed them - but she needed to talk to someone.

SITTING ALONE in the room while Tyler went on two solo dates and another group date had been torture, and she couldn't even commiserate with Maryanne. Plus, the women made sure to brag about how great the date had gone when they'd returned. Laney had no idea if it was truth or not, but it was still hard to listen to. She'd spent a lot of time reading and praying, but God hadn't given her any grand revelations and her fears that maybe this had been a mistake were still alive and well.

. . .

LANEY STARED at the clothes in her small wardrobe. Justin had said dress casual, but that could literally mean anything, and she hadn't always been privy to what Tyler's dates would be even as his makeup artist. She decided on a pair of Capri pants and her favorite Toby Mac t-shirt. At least she would be comfortable whatever they threw at her.

"TIME TO GO," Cassidy said sticking her head in the door.

"THANKS." Cassidy had been the nicest one to her so far although even that had just been civility.

She followed Cassidy out of the house and to the limo where Erica and Kanina were waiting.

MARYANNE AND JUSTIN also stood outside the limo. Laney wanted to sit next to her friend just for a friendly word of encouragement, but she thought that might make the women dislike her even more, so she didn't. She flashed a small smile and climbed in the limo allowing the other women to sit closer to Tyler.

"ARE YOU LADIES READY?" he asked as the door shut. He glanced to each woman, but Laney thought he stared the longest at her. She couldn't believe she hadn't seen him since the ceremony.

. . .

"What are we doing?" Cassidy asked.

"Something I haven't done in ages." Tyler's lips pulled into a mischievous grin. "It involves music and wheels."

Music and wheels? Were they going to an arcade? Some games had steering wheels, but Laney couldn't remember if there was music. It had been ages since she'd been to an arcade. Or perhaps a go-cart track? Again wheels, but she didn't remember music.

Her heart sank when they pulled up to a roller-skating rink. Laney hadn't been on skates in years and that was mainly because she had no coordination on them. She fell more often than not or spent the time clinging to the rail. For a second, she wondered if Justin knew of her lack of coordination and had planned the whole thing, but surely that was silly.

"Cool, I haven't been skating in years," Kanina said.

. . .

Cassidy laughed. "I'm on a roller derby team so this is old hat for me."

Of course, it was. Laney knew Tyler had connected with Cassidy, and she began to wonder if maybe Cassidy wouldn't be a better match.

"I always loved skating, especially the couple's skate." Erica put her hand on Tyler's thigh and smiled up at him as she spoke. Laney wanted to slap her hand away, but she tucked her hands under her lap and gritted her teeth. She could get through this date.

"You okay?" Maryanne asked softly as they made their way toward the door of the rink.

"I don't skate," Laney whispered back quietly. Maryanne's eyes widened in realization, and she offered a sympathetic nose scrunch before hurrying ahead to set up.

Laney was the last one to approach the counter and ask for her skates. She hated having to ask for shoes in her size. More than one person in her life had told her she had big feet for a girl, especially since she wasn't extraordinarily tall. "Size ten please."

Sure enough, the kid manning the counter looked at her, raised an eyebrow, but thankfully said nothing as he turned to the massive shelving unit that housed the roller skates. He plucked a pair and handed them across the table to her.

Laney tried not to think about how many other feet had been in the skates as she took them over to the table Tyler and the other girls were at. She wasn't generally a germaphobe and she knew they sprayed them but still they were rental shoes and they were old. People had been putting their smelly feet in these skates for decades. Who knew if they had athlete's foot or some other foot fungus that might survive through whatever the employees sprayed in them.

She took off her shoes and slid her feet in. The sole was knobby and worn and the laces were uneven. Laney was only able to lace her left skate three quarters of the way up. She hoped it would do. Breaking an ankle would be embarrassing to say the least.

. . .

"You okay there?" Tyler's voice was warm and inviting. It surprised Laney that he had stayed by her. Cassidy, Erica, and Kanina were already out in the rink looking as if they skated every day.

"I'm not very good on skates," she said as she tried to stand. One foot slipped forward while the other slipped back and her body lunged forward. She grabbed onto Tyler's shirt to keep herself from falling and his arms stole around her in support. "I'm sorry."

"Don't be," he said with a smile, "just the fact that you are trying is amazing."

"Tyler come on. Let's see what you got." Cassidy curled her finger at him in a 'come hither' gesture as she skated backwards across the rink. Effortlessly it seemed.

"Go on," Laney said when Tyler looked back to her. "I'll make it out there eventually. Just save me a skate."

"You got it." He flashed her a wide smile, made sure she was steady on her feet, and then zipped off toward Cassidy.

. . .

How could she be the only one with zero coordination on skates? Laney tried to push off, but she could feel her balance tilting again. She grabbed the table until she centered herself then decided to step instead of skate her way to the rink. It was slow going, but she finally made it there. She grasped the rail as if it were a lifeline and pulled herself along it. The cold metal felt clammy against her hand or was that her hand that was clammy?

"Guess we'll see who Tyler favors now, huh?" Erica asked as she skated by Laney. Laney shook her head and continued inching around the rink.

"Okay, all you couples. Grab hands and let's do our first couple skate," a voice said over the loudspeaker. The lights went dark and spots began circulating around the floor. Great. Now, she had to try to skate in the dark. As she turned to see who Tyler was choosing for the first skate, her hand hit something slimy on the rail. She jerked her hand back sending her balance off. Laney saw her skate fly up in the air and had just enough time to find that odd before she fell backward, and the world went dark.

TYLER WATCHED Laney fall as if in slow motion. Her hand jerked up with such force that her body arched backward. Her right leg lifted in the air followed by the left, and her arms flailed but not in a way to break her fall. The first thing to hit the floor was her butt followed by her head hitting the rail. That was bad, but when her head bounced off the rail and hit the hard rink floor, he knew she was unconscious. Whether she had blacked out from fear or from the concussion he was sure she had, he wasn't positive, but neither was good.

"GO FIND A PHONE AND CALL 911," he said to Erica whose eyes had widened to the size of quarters. She nodded and skated off and he turned back to Laney. Tyler was glad to see Cassidy already by her side. As a firefighter, she probably had some paramedic training.

"IS SHE OKAY?"

CASSIDY LOOKED UP AT HIM. "I don't know for sure. She hit her head pretty hard. Have you called an ambulance?"

"I SENT ERICA." He placed a hand on Laney's forehead surprised at the emotions racing through him. Had he really only known her a few weeks? Her eyes fluttered open and she jerked as if trying to sit up. "Don't move," he said even as Cassidy pushed gently on her shoulders. "You hit your head and we need to have you checked out."

"It seems I do that a lot around you," she said softly before her eyes closed again.

Tyler bit back his grin. Smiling seemed inappropriate right now, but she was right. In the short time he had known her, she had fallen into his arms, into his chin, and now this. On most women, this would be annoying, maybe even cause for alarm, but he found it endearing on Laney.

The paramedics arrived a few minutes later and forced Tyler to stand back and watch as they loaded her up on a stretcher. Watching her get taped down stirred his heart in a way he hadn't felt in a long time.

"I'm going with her," he said to the paramedics. They nodded and began walking toward the exit. Tyler turned to the other women and Maryanne. "Can you make sure they get back all right?"

Maryanne nodded. Fear flooded her eyes, but he could tell

she was trying to be brave. "Make sure they take good care of her."

Tyler flashed a tight smile before jogging to catch up with the paramedics. As he climbed up in the ambulance, he took ahold of Laney's hand. *Please Lord, let her be okay.*

Minutes later, they were entering the hospital. "Twenty-eight-year-old woman fell and hit her head at the roller rink. Woke briefly before we arrived. Vital signs are good."

The doctor looked around catching eyes with Tyler. "Do you know her name?"

"Laney. Laney Swann. She's-" He stopped unsure how to finish that sentence. She wasn't really his girlfriend though she probably would be outside this crazy scenario.

"Laney Swann?" The doctor looked back down at Laney as the paramedics transferred her to a bed and then back to Tyler. "Do you know if she's from Texas?"

"She is." Tyler wasn't sure how much information he

should give out, but this doctor was acting as if he knew her, and he didn't think confirming the question was crossing any lines. "Why?"

THE DOCTOR SMILED. "We went to high school together. I'll take good care of her, but I need you to wait outside." He pointed to the waiting room. Tyler wanted to object, but the doctor had already closed the curtain.

As HE WALKED over to the chairs, Tyler wondered how close they had been in high school. He hadn't had the chance to ask her much about her past and though he knew it was probably an unfounded fear, he worried there might be something between them. A doctor was more successful than a rancher by most people's standards and women seemed to leave him for more successful men most of the time. Tyler just hoped Laney was different.

LANEY OPENED her eyes surprised to see white. Where was she? Oh, right, she'd fallen at the rink. Probably made a huge fool of herself as she did it too. That explained the ache in her head, but why did her butt hurt so badly?

"HEY, WELCOME BACK."

. . .

Laney looked to the left where a handsome man in a white coat was monitoring something on a computer screen. He looked familiar, but Laney couldn't quite place him. Probably because of the pain in her head. Or the fact she could only see his profile. Or both.

"How are you feeling?"

"Like I've been hit by a truck."

"More like a metal railing and a concrete floor." He smiled as he turned to face her, and Laney's breath caught.

"Dallas?"

His grin widened. "I wondered if you would remember me. What are the odds, huh?"

Would she remember him? That was a stupid question. She'd spent four years of high school pining after him and he'd been part of the reason she had gone into makeup art. "Pretty crazy, I'd say. I can't believe you're a doctor."

"Yeah, I thought I wanted to be an engineer, but then I ended up taking an anatomy course in college for some credit I needed and found that I loved it. I'm still in my residency, but I can't see myself doing anything else now."

Laney would have nodded if her head hadn't hurt so bad. She seemed incapable of any words at the moment. Dallas Nixon was here. He was her doctor, and he was just as handsome as she remembered, but she didn't feel the sparks she remembered in high school. There were no fireworks, no rapid heartbeat. Was that because it had been so long since she had seen him or because of Tyler?

"What are you doing in California? And what were you doing at a roller rink?"

"I doubt you would believe me," Laney said. The whole thing sounded ridiculous to her and she had been there. "I was asked to do make up for a reality TV show and now I'm a contestant."

. . .

"On the show?" Dallas's eyebrow rose an inch and his voice held a note of incredulity.

"Yeah, I know. I'm not really the contestant type."

"So, the guy who came in with you…." His voice trailed off as if he was trying to make the connection and then realization sparked in his eyes. "It's a dating show."

Laney hated the way he said it, like she was desperate for a date. Of course, that's what she had thought about the contestants initially too, so she couldn't really blame him. "It is, but it's not like you think."

He took her hand and squeezed it. "Well, whatever it is, I'm glad I was the doctor on duty when you came in. It was good to see you again."

The door opened then, and Tyler stepped in. Though Dallas let go of her hand almost immediately, she saw Tyler's jaw tense. He had seen it, and he didn't look happy about it. "How is she doing, doctor?"

. . .

DALLAS GLANCED at Tyler before returning his attention to Laney, but now she almost wished he wouldn't. The tension in the room was palpable. "She is fine. You had a mild concussion and you bruised your tailbone, so you'll need to take it easy for the next few weeks, but you'll recover fully. You'll probably also need a donut pillow to sit with for a while, so I'll have the nurse bring that in. I'd like to keep you overnight for observation, but you should be fine to go tomorrow. I have to check on some other patients, but I'll be back to look in on you later. Push the call button if you need anything." He gave her one final smile before exiting the room.

TYLER CROSSED to her bed and took her hand. "I'm glad to hear you're going to be okay. It worried me when I saw you fall."

"I'M sorry I worried you. I should have warned you about my klutzy tendency. If this changes how you feel, I understand."

"LANEY," he took her hand, "it changes nothing in how I feel. I don't care if you can't skate, but I do have to ask. Is there anything between you and the doctor?"

. . .

Laney shook her head. "Dallas was my crush in high school, but he never gave me the time of day. He was just being friendly."

Tyler's eyes searched hers as if deciding if he could trust her, but finally he nodded. "I'm glad to hear it because I have to tell you that my heart froze when I saw you fall. I don't know why I feel so close to you in this short time, but I do."

"I do too, and I agree it's crazy, but it might just be a God thing."

His lips pulled up in a smile. "Maybe it is. God gave me peace about coming on the show, and I know things always work out better when I let Him be in control, but it isn't always easy."

"No, it isn't." Laney thought back to all her failed relationships and her job with Madame Bonavich. She hadn't been letting God control her life; she'd been trying to control her life. No wonder it hadn't worked out the way she'd planned, but as she looked at Tyler, she realized God's way was a lot better. Laney wanted him to kiss her, but she didn't want their first kiss to be in a hospital room, and it appeared he didn't either as he sucked in a breath and then released it.

"I have to get back to the house, but I'll be here when you get released."

"I'm not going anywhere," she said with a smile, but she hated that he was going back to the house. She hated knowing there was another ceremony and three other women who would visit his ranch. She couldn't wait for this show to be over.

19

*T*yler pondered his options the whole ride home. He didn't want to continue this game any longer. It wasn't fair to the remaining women, and it wasn't fair to Laney. The question was - how did he get out of it?

"Well, you really know how to throw a wrench in things," Justin said as soon as the limo pulled up to the house.

"What do you mean?" Tyler asked. "I had to make sure she was okay."

"Of course, you did, but we showed the footage to our focus group. None of them want you to choose anyone else now, so we can't air it without risking the audience reacting the exact same way. At least not her fall."

"Okay, so don't air her fall." Tyler couldn't care less what they did. Watching Laney fall confirmed his suspicions. He wanted her and no one else.

"The problem is, if we don't, we'd have to re-film the

episode which would be fine, but I doubt Laney wants to go roller skating again when she gets out. A possibility of choosing something else exists, but honestly, she's going to be slower and in pain. She won't be her normal self and people will wonder why."

Tyler blew out a breath of frustrated air. "Okay Justin, so what do you propose?"

Justin's eyes gleamed and he nodded. "Exactly."

"What?"

"Propose. To her. At the next ceremony. The audience will be so in love with the two of you after this episode that they won't care if it takes three episodes out. This will be something new and unexpected. They'll eat it up."

"But what about those three episodes? Won't you have to do something for them?"

Justin waved a hand. "We'll fill them. We can still film her going to your ranch. Then you'll meet her family. We can have a women-tell-all episode, or," his eyes lit up, "we'll film an episode of the two of you meeting with our wedding planner to plan the wedding-"

"Wait, what? Justin, I care about her, but we've only known each other a few weeks. That's a little early to get married."

"Relax. You don't have to get married right away. Simply start the process. The audience loves a good love story and yours will be epic. We'll run teasers every few months. There will be a new Cowboy series running by then too which will keep them happy until your televised wedding."

"Televised? What if Laney doesn't want a televised wedding?" He wasn't even sure he did. This reality show had been enough television for him for a lifetime.

"Don't worry, we're going to make it worth both of your while."

"But we haven't even kissed. Is the audience really going to buy I want to marry her without even kissing her?"

"So, take care of that. We'll arrange some alone time when you pick her up from the hospital. Make it happen then. Look, I know you're tired of the game. She will be too after this. This is a good deal, Tyler."

"Let me pray on it. I'm assuming you don't want me to tell Laney - surprise emotion and all that, right?" Tyler hated that he was beginning to understand the manipulation needed for ratings.

"Now you're starting to get it. Look, if it makes you feel better, we can go over the details with her after she accepts the proposal. I have no doubt that she will."

Nothing about this whole situation made Tyler feel better except no longer having to string the other women along. "Fine. I'll get back to you."

"Everything looks good, Laney. You'll need to take it easy, and you might have headaches for a few weeks. I've prescribed some extra strength Tylenol for you should you need it."

Laney took the prescription paper and smiled up at Dallas. "Thank you, I appreciate it."

He flashed her a wide smile. "Well, it is my job, but hey, if things don't work out with your reality star-"

Laney shook her head. "He's not a reality star, not really. He's a rancher in Texas, but if things don't work out, I'll definitely look you up."

"Okay. I'll hold you to that. I can't release you till your ride gets here, but I'll have the nurse print up your discharge papers."

As Laney watched him walk away, a sense of wonder fluttered through her. Ten years she had held a torch for Dallas and now she felt nothing. Well, not entirely nothing. He was still handsome, but it appeared her heart now belonged to another. Now if she were just sure his heart belonged to her as well.

She wondered if they had filmed the ceremony and tried not to be jealous. She knew he would choose her for one of the dates at his ranch, but three other girls would also get that date. However, she couldn't focus on that. She needed to focus on the prize at the end–the possibility that Tyler would choose her, and they would get to develop a better connection.

Tyler appeared in her doorway. "Hey, you ready to get out of here?"

She smiled at him. "Am I ever."

The nurse entered a moment later with the discharge papers and a round air filled pillow. "It's not sexy, but it will make sitting bearable for short periods of time anyway. Try not to sit for too long. Get up and walk around."

"Got it." Laney couldn't believe the nurse was telling her all of this in front of Tyler. As if her fall hadn't been embarrassing enough, now she could add this humiliation to her growing list.

"Butt pillow," she said holding it up as she gathered her things. "That ought to make a great story for our kids one day." The words were out of her mouth before she fully realized what she was saying. When it clicked, her eyes widened. Oh gravy, had she just assumed they were going to marry and have children?

Tyler didn't even bat an eye. With a wide smile, he fired back at her. "With your klutzy tendencies, they will probably issue a helmet to our kids at birth."

Laney took his hand and the corners of her mouth split into a wide grin. "I like the sound of that."

"What? Helmets? How bad is this klutzy tendency?"

"No," she batted his arm with a playful swat, "the word 'our.' It sounds good."

He squeezed her hand as they walked down the hall. "Yeah, it sure does."

Laney forced herself not to grimace as she sat down gingerly on the donut in the back of the limo.

"Is it bad?" Tyler asked as he turned to her.

"It's kind of like sitting on a really pointy rock all the time." She shifted around to try to get comfortable.

"Well, you won't have to sit too long, I promise."

Laney wondered what that meant. She had assumed

they were simply returning to the house as Justin had said they wouldn't have any solo dates until Tyler's ranch, so a feeling of surprise blossomed when the limo pulled up to the beach. "What's this?"

His eyes twinkled, and his lips twitched. "Justin said we could have a little alone time on the way back today, and since sitting is so painful, I thought a walk on the beach might be more fun." He stepped out first and then reached back for her.

"You thought right." She laced her fingers through his and matched his mischievous grin. "I'm not sure I'm allowed to ask, but how did your other dates go?" Laney wasn't sure she wanted to hear the answer, but she was hoping for a little reassurance. What had started as attraction was quickly blossoming into real feelings.

He shook his head. "Nope, this time is about us. I want to know more about you."

Laney could appreciate that. She firmly believed God had brought them together, but a lasting relationship needed a firm foundation, and, in that area, they were lacking. "Okay, what do you want to know?"

"You said once you became a makeup artist, so you wouldn't be invisible. What made you think you were invisible?"

"Phew, that is quite the question. When I was in school, I was smart. In sixth grade, I won the Valedictorian award, but I wanted to be more than smart, you know? I wanted, like so many girls, to be popular. And I tried everything - buying the right clothes, wearing the right makeup, but I was the girl everyone knew but no one invited out. Looking back now, I realize God was probably protecting me. Several of the popular girls in my class ended up pregnant before graduation, and one even committed suicide after her mother forced her to have an abortion, but I couldn't see that then. All I could see was the girl that no one wanted to date, and so I thought about what would make me stand out. I watched a modeling show and figured if I could learn makeup then I could make myself beautiful and if I were good enough at it, I could do makeup for models and make a name for myself. That's stupid, right?"

He pulled her to a stop and turned her to face him. His eyes tore into her soul as his hands cupped her face. "It's not stupid because it's how you felt, but you are beautiful. And you don't need makeup or a name. You just need a man who sees you, and I see you Laney."

The sounds of the beach faded as Laney stared into his eyes. So much depth resided in those blue jewels - warmth and tenderness and strength. Her heartbeat grew louder pounding in her head, and Laney's breath stilled. Electricity crackled between them sending arcs down to her toes. She wanted to kiss him. She wanted to feel his cheek against her own. Rough or stubbly she didn't care, and as if he could read her mind, his face drew closer to hers until she could feel his breath on her face. His lips parted, and she closed her eyes.

A fire burned through her body at the touch of his lips. Hot and cold and a hundred other things she had never felt raced through her veins. Her hands wound around his neck and into his hair. His hair was soft against her fingertips. As the kiss deepened, she needed more of him, and she pulled on his neck. Her body molded into his and a flame of desire ricocheted through her. A flame that was so hot she needed to douse it before she compromised her morals.

She loosened her grip on his neck and, as if sensing her desires, he pulled back ending the kiss. For a moment they stared at each other, no words existing. Then Laney opened her mouth not even sure what would come out. "I see you too, and you're enough." She wasn't sure why she added the last three words except that she felt he needed to hear them. Just as she needed to be seen, he needed to know he was enough, and he was.

20

Tyler's hand touched the ring box in his pocket again. The producers had taken him to their private designer the day before and he'd picked out the perfect ring for Laney. The jeweler's selection was all beautiful, but Tyler knew when he laid eyes on the princess cut diamond that it was the one for her.

He hadn't even gotten to see her much after their kiss on the beach, but a part of him was glad. Every time he thought about her, he wanted to kiss her again, and Tyler knew he would have if he'd had any alone time with her, but Justin made sure that didn't happen.

Instead, Justin tried to keep him busy with shopping and helping to edit some of the footage including the kiss with Laney. Maryanne had been quite a distance away when the kiss happened, but the distance hadn't affected the heat. It looked as passionate on screen as it had been in real life. And now he was only minutes away from getting to kiss her again.

The women filed in, and Tyler marveled at their acting ability. Even though none of them knew of his proposal, they all understood Laney was the only woman for him. Yet they still wore hopeful nervous expressions as they walked in.

"Welcome ladies," Justin said when all the women were settled. "Tonight will be the final elimination ceremony. There are ten of you, but Tyler only has four hats. Remember if he does not give you a hat you must say your goodbyes and exit the house. Tyler, when you're ready."

Tyler picked up a hat and smiled out at the women. Justin had given him a prepared speech to memorize and while the gesture annoyed Tyler at first, he was glad now. His own thoughts were failing him as he looked out at Laney. "Ladies, first let me say that it has been a pleasure getting to know you all. This journey is not an easy one as there are things about each of you I have come to adore, but I had to make a decision on those I envisioned in my life long term." He took a breath, no longer sure if it was for added effect or because he needed it. "Laney."

As she made her way to him, joy burst inside him, and he couldn't help but grin at her. "Laney from the day I met you when you first fell into my arms to the day you fell at the rink, you have stood out to me. Your sweet spirit shines through in all you do and captured my heart. So, I have to ask you…" his right hand went to his pocket and he grabbed the box, "will you marry me?" In one motion, he pulled the box out, dropped to his knees, and flipped the lid.

Behind her, every woman's jaw dropped. Tyler had no idea if they were acting or truly shocked, but he didn't care. His attention was on the woman in front of him whose mouth had parted to accept his hat and now hung suspended as she stared at the ring.

Her eyes darted to his and the questions swam in them. She wanted to know if he was serious. With a slight nod, he reassured her, and her lips folded into a huge smile.

"Yes, Tyler, of course I will marry you."

As Tyler slid the beautiful ring on Laney's hand, the surrealness hit. He had just proposed to a woman he had only known for a few weeks, and she had accepted. How was that possible? But he knew the answer to that. If God was in control of this relationship, then time was only a number.

"Congratulations Laney," Justin said, and the girls behind echoed his sentiments. "I know this season ended a little early, but don't worry, we have a few more episodes up our sleeves. Join us next week as Laney travels to Tyler's ranch to meet his friends and make sure the ranching life is one she can live with. Then we'll travel to Laney's house and meet her family, and if we're lucky, maybe we'll be airing their wedding in the future."

Justin's game show face disappeared when the cameras stopped rolling and he became all business. "All right, ladies, you can get packed up. We'll be reaching out to you about the Maui show. I'm sorry things didn't work out this time, but that is the nature of this business. Laney, Tyler, we should talk about the filming schedule for the next two weeks."

Tyler pulled Laney to him and kissed her forehead. "Sure, Justin, we can do that, but do you think we could just have a minute or two to celebrate?" This whole show had been a whirlwind blowing him from one place to the next, and he just needed a moment to catch his breath and to steal another kiss from the woman who had just agreed to be his wife.

21

Nancy's eyes widened as she opened the door and before even saying hello, she turned and hollered back into the house. "Aaron, get out here. It's Tyler." She pulled him in for a fierce hug.

"I guess you've been watching," he said with a chuckle.

"Of course I have. Now when do we get to meet this Laney?" She glanced around as if looking for the cameras.

Tyler laughed. "There's no camera today, but how can you be certain Laney is coming?" The final episode hadn't aired yet. He wasn't even sure if the episode of their disastrous group date had aired.

She waved her hand in a dismissive gesture. "Don't be ridiculous. I could tell from the first time you guys interacted that she was the one for you. I probably knew before you did." She punched him lightly on the arm before pulling him inside.

He fixed her with a narrowed gaze after shutting the

door behind him. "How? As far as I know the first time we interacted together with the cameras running was the group date."

She raised her eyebrow at him? "You don't know?"

"Evidently not. Though I'm not sure *what* I don't know. Please fill me in."

"Tyler, before the episode that Laney joined the contestants, they aired half an hour of footage of the two of you. The day you met, the limo ride before the beach date, that moment in your main room when I was almost certain you were going to kiss her." She placed her hands on her hips and raised her brow at him. "Why didn't you kiss her?"

Tyler sighed and ignored her question. He'd known there were cameras in the house, but he'd had no idea they were in his room or the limo. Nor had he known they had been recording the whole time, but it made sense. After working with Justin and Peter, he would put nothing past them. "Okay, so you saw that footage, but still, how could you possibly know I chose Laney?"

"Because I'm not stupid. I saw that look in your eye - the same one I saw in Aaron's eye when I knew he had decided to propose to me. It was the look of a man in love." She wagged her finger at him and wiggled her eyebrows.

"You don't think it's too soon to propose? I mean it's only been a few weeks." Even though he had already popped the question, he wanted to know Nancy's thoughts before she knew of the proposal.

She crossed her arms and fixed him with an even gaze. "First of all, there's no such thing. When you know, you know, and God's hand was pretty evident in all of this, but for argument's sake, let me ask you something."

He bit back a smile. He had missed Nancy and her no-nonsense approach to things. "Okay, shoot."

"Is she the first thing you think of when you wake up? The last thing you think of before you go to sleep?"

"Of course, but-"

"Can you picture your life with her?" He rolled his eyes. "Okay, now can you imagine life without her?"

Even though he had already proposed, that stopped him, and he paused to think. He could see Laney in his life for sure, but the thought of continuing in life without her held no appeal.

"That." She pointed at his face. "That is how I know you've decided. Now, let me see the ring."

Tyler laughed and shook his head. "I don't have it."

"I don't believe that for a second. Anyone with half a brain knows you already bought it." She lunged forward as if about to pat him down or tackle him to the ground. Tyler wasn't sure which.

He shrugged and stepped away from her hands, enjoying stringing her along for a moment. "I didn't buy a ring."

"Hey man, good to have you back. You are back, right?" Aaron entered the living room and crossed to Tyler holding out his hand for a shake.

"I am. Well, I have one more episode to film elsewhere, but otherwise, I am."

"When do we get to meet Laney?"

Nancy smiled at her husband before shooting a triumphant look at Tyler. "That's what I said."

"You'll get to meet her soon."

"Good, because I've known since the first time they showed her that she was the one for you. I was hoping you wouldn't be so dense that you'd miss that she cared about you. You had me worried for a few of those episodes."

"It's not a normal situation."

"Well, why don't you tell us all about it over dinner? I made spaghetti." Nancy linked her arm through his and lead the way to the kitchen.

Tyler couldn't help grinning. It was so good to be home. He had really missed Aaron and Nancy the last few weeks, and he too couldn't wait for them to meet Laney.

Laney gingerly stepped out of the limo and grabbed her donut pillow. She couldn't believe she still had to carry the thing around nearly two weeks after her fall, but her booty was still sore if she sat for too long. Tyler stood at the bottom step of his house grinning at her and looking devastatingly handsome in a pair of jeans and his cowboy hat. She hadn't seen him in over a week - they had kept Laney working for another show while they sent Tyler back to his ranch to get caught up. The distance had been hard, but they had called each other and begun a video devotional a few times a week.

"How's the tuchus?" he teased as he walked toward her.

"Healing nicely, thank you very much. I should be fine as long as you don't expect me to go trail riding today."

His lips twisted into a grimace. "Ooh, my friends live in the back country and the only way to get there is by horseback."

"Very funny," she said as she punched him in the arm.

He caught her hand on the way back and pulled her to his chest. His arms wound around her waist, and her breath caught. "There's still a camera, you know?" She indicated Maryanne with a nod of her head.

"I don't care. I've been waiting too long to do this again."

His head lowered, and his lips pressed down on hers sending a flame of desire all the way down to her toes. Her arms wound around his neck and she leaned into him enjoying the heat that burned between them. Laney had a hard time catching her breath when the kiss ended. "Well, with welcome kisses like that, I might have to go away more often."

"Don't you dare," he whispered in her ear before pulling back. "Come on, let me show you the ranch and then I'll take you to meet Aaron and Nancy." He laced his fingers through hers as he led her up the stairs and onto the porch. "One day, I want to have a big wraparound porch here with a rocker or a swing and a table."

"Breakfast on the porch?" She'd never one growing up in the city, but she'd always thought they sounded nice. The closest she'd ever gotten was a tiny balcony, big enough to fit a single chair, in one apartment she lived in. Unfortunately, when she'd sat and tried to drink her coffee in the morning, the sound of the traffic and honking had made it a less than peaceful experience.

Here though, she could see it. Tyler's plot of land was expansive and there were no neighbors as far as the eye could see. She wondered if she'd be able to handle the quiet.

He didn't take her on a full tour as she needed to be able to ride for that, but he showed her the house, the barn, and enough of the ranch to leave her in awe. The place was large, larger than any apartment she had lived in. Laney had no idea how to quantify a rancher's success, but she thought he'd done well for himself.

"Ready to go meet the woman who brought us together?" he asked when they returned to the front of the house. Laney nodded. She had wanted to meet Nancy since he first spoke of her.

Nancy and Aaron's house was even bigger than Tyler's and Laney could see why he wanted the wrap-around porch. They had one, and it was beautiful. Tyler laced his fingers through hers and flashed her a smile before ringing the doorbell.

A woman, dressed simply in flannel and jeans, opened the door. Her eyes lit up when she saw Tyler and Laney assumed it had to be Nancy.

"Hey Nancy. I'd like you to meet Laney."

Nancy turned her warm brown eyes on Laney, and the look she sent made Laney feel as if they'd been friends forever. "Laney, it is so nice to meet you."

"You as well. I didn't think I would ever meet anyone on a reality tv show, but I'm certainly glad you made Tyler audition." She looked up at Tyler and smiled still unsure of how she'd ended up with him.

"I want to hear all about what didn't air live or on the cameras. Tyler told me some, but you know how men are - they miss all the best details." She flashed a conspiratorial smile at Tyler before grabbing Laney's arm and leading her into the house.

"Don't mind me. I'll just go find Aaron and discuss things without details."

"Okay so spill. I want to know when you first fell for Tyler."

Laney laughed at Nancy's excited demeanor. She was like a kid tasting candy for the first time. "Well, it would probably be when I literally fell into his arms or he caught my fall, rather."

Nancy laughed. "You do seem to fall a lot near him."

"I'm not usually that big of a klutz, but his eyes...." She trailed off unsure exactly how to put into words what his eyes were, but Nancy seemed to understand. As Laney continued to answer Nancy's questions, she knew they would be good friends.

"Okay, you have to meet my husband, Aaron. He'll

never admit it, but I think he's just as excited to meet you as I was."

Laney chuckled as she followed Nancy outside. She couldn't remember the last time anyone had been so excited to meet her.

Aaron was a man of average build with warm brown eyes just like Nancy's. "You must be Laney," he said as he pulled her for a hug. "It's so nice to meet you."

It was a good thing Laney wasn't opposed to hugging as Tyler's friends seemed intent on it. "It's nice to meet you too. I'd say I've heard so much about you, but I haven't."

Aaron feigned a hurt expression and turned to Tyler. "Really man? Not a word?"

Tyler shrugged and flashed a wink at Laney. "It was an odd situation."

"So, you keep saying. Speaking of which when is the big day?"

Laney looked to Tyler surprised to see his jaw tighten. "Oh, we haven't talked about it yet much less set a date."

"Actually, the date is in four months." Tyler's voice sounded pained and tight.

Laney's head shot forward. "What?"

The color drained from his face. "They didn't tell you? Justin said he would talk to you about the contract."

"Contract? What contract? Are you getting paid to marry me?" Her arms folded across her chest as her defensive wall began to build.

"It's not like that," Tyler began.

"No? Then why don't you tell me what it is like. I

accepted your proposal because I care for you and wanted to get to know you better. Even though we haven't known each other long, I felt like we were supposed to be together, but now you're telling me you signed a contract to marry me?" Her voice rose in pitch at the end. Laney hated the sound of it but seemed powerless to stop it.

"Hear me out, Laney. After your fall, I didn't want to continue, but I had signed the initial contract. Proposing to you and letting them film the wedding was the compromise. I didn't know they hadn't told you."

Though his words made sense, Laney's insecurities had reared their ugly heads again making her question everything - the timing, their feelings, the future. "Excuse me. I need a minute." Laney pulled open the sliding glass door and stormed through the house. She didn't stop until she had stepped through the front door and was on the porch.

The air had cooled as the sun set and she shivered from the chill, but she didn't go back inside. Instead she sat on the porch swing letting the bite in the air sharpen her thoughts. She'd thought the hard part would be over now that the show was finished, but it appeared the truly hard part was just beginning.

"Hey, you okay?" Maryanne stood in the doorway without her camera.

Laney had gotten so used to the camera following her everywhere for the past few weeks that she had forgotten Maryanne had even been in the room, but she was thankful it was her friend who had come out to check on her instead of Tyler or Nancy.

"I don't know. I mean I know I care for him, but-"

"But this feels fast."

Laney nodded and grabbed her necklace. It was a simple cross, and she was so used to wearing it that she often forgot it was there, but whenever she felt really stressed, rubbing her thumb across the design always seemed to calm her down.

Maryanne shook her head as she sat next to Laney on the swing. "I know it's hard, but he's not Brian, Laney."

"Brian? What do you mean? Don't you mean Dallas?"

"No, I mean Brian. You don't remember?" Laney shook her head. "Freshman year before you set your sights on Dallas, you liked a boy named Brian. Maybe I remember because I had just met you and you talked about him all the time. I thought you were a little boy crazy."

Laney snorted. She probably had been boy crazy, but most teenage girls were.

"Anyway, one day he asked you out in a note or something. You were so excited because you were supposed to meet after school and walk to the local hangout."

"But when I arrived at the meeting spot, he told me it had been a joke." Laney said the words slowly as the memory came back to her. She had forgotten, or maybe blocked, that painful memory. "Thanks for the walk down memory lane, but why would you bring that up?"

"Because I think your lack of faith in men stems from this interaction with Brian. I mean look at your track record after that incident. Less than a month later, you declared your crush on Dallas. You focused all your attention on a boy who was not attainable."

Laney opened her mouth to argue. Not attainable might be a little bit of a stretch. True, she had been invisible in high school, but Dallas had flirted with her at the hospital. However, before she could utter a word, Maryanne continued.

"I think you focused on Dallas because you were afraid of getting hurt again, and if he never asked you out, he could never hurt you. Now you are afraid that Tyler has ulterior motives, but he's not Brian. I've watched him with you. He loves you, and this reality show made your relationship different. It made it public and fast and maybe a little messy, but that's not always a bad thing. I've been doing this show a long time, and I've watched all the relationships. You know how I know you two will be okay?"

"How?"

"Because you have the one thing the other couple had who lasted."

"What's that?"

"Your faith. All these couples that fail have nothing to stand on. They meet, they're attracted, some I think even fall in love, but when they get out into the real world, they have nothing grounding them. No common goal. You guys do. Like the other couple who lasted, you two have your faith in God. You both know that putting God first is the key to any successful relationship, and so what if he gets a little more money for proposing when he did? You got something too, right?"

Though it pained her, Laney nodded. She had taken something in exchange for agreeing to become a contestant. Tyler's wasn't any worse.

Maryanne didn't say 'I told you so," but it was written all over her face. "I thought so. Besides, this money they are giving him benefits you as well. It's money to help his ranch - a place you'll probably be living at soon."

Laney stared at her friend. When had she become so wise? In high school, Jennifer had been the outspoken one of the group who was always offering advice, but either Maryanne had been listening or she'd grown a lot in the past ten years. "Did you major in psychology?"

Maryanne laughed. "No but working in the entertainment industry gives me plenty of opportunities to dispense my wonderful advice. Now, come on, why don't we go back inside, eat that wonderful smelling dinner, and find out what else is in the contract?"

Laney still had her reservations, but Maryanne's words did make sense. "Okay, let's go."

22

Tyler took a deep breath and adjusted his hat as he stepped out of the limo. The nerves in his stomach fluttered like a kite in the wind, and he wondered if Laney had been as nervous meeting his friends as he was meeting her family. He hadn't expected to be nervous, but Laney's reaction at his ranch had made him wonder if her family might feel the same.

"Don't worry, they'll love you," Laney said as if sensing his unease. She linked her arm through his and led the way up the pathway. Maryanne followed a step behind giving them a little privacy.

Perhaps that was part of the added pressure. Not only was he meeting Laney's family for the first time, but it would be filmed and the whole world would see it. Well, not the whole world, but the whole 'Who Wants to Marry a Cowboy' fan base which he had found out was quite large and opinionated.

Laney pushed open the front door of the two-story house and called out, "Mom, Dad, we're here." She removed her coat and hung it on a coat rack which sat just to the side of the door indicating he should do the same.

He glanced around the room as he shrugged out of his duster. It appeared to be a formal living room. The couch and chair surrounded a small coffee table and a raised lamp flanked them. Probably a reading area as there was no television in the room though an old piano sat along the wall.

A woman who could have been an older version of Laney appeared in the doorway at the far end of the room. She had the same blond hair and brown eyes. Her face held a few more wrinkles, but she had aged gracefully and could easily have been mistaken for Laney's older sister. She smiled at the sight of them and glided across the floor.

"Laney, it's so good to have you home," she said pulling Laney in for a hug. Then she turned her gaze on Tyler and his nerves fluttered faster. "And you must be Tyler. I've heard so much about you." She kept the smile on her face, but Tyler could hear the hint of apprehension in her voice.

"Mostly good, I hope," he said as he took her proffered hand. "It's a pleasure to meet you, ma'am."

"Well, come on in. David, Laney's father, is in the back living room."

She led the way through a pristine kitchen and into a larger living room. This one was filled with comfortable furniture, a television surrounded by bookshelves, and a large man in a chair cleaning a gun. Tyler wasn't quite sure whether he should laugh or take off running.

"Dad. What are you doing?" Shock and anger threaded Laney's voice, but they didn't faze the man.

"I'm just cleaning my gun. Figured if I was going to meet the man who proposed to my daughter after a few weeks without even meeting us first, I should be prepared for all contingencies."

"I am so sorry," Laney said shaking her head.

Tyler figured laughter was the better option, and he smiled and stepped toward her father. "That's quite all right, Laney. I can understand his position. When I have a daughter, I'll probably be just as protective." He held out his hand to the man. "Tyler Hall, sir. Pleasure to meet you, and I apologize for the crazy circumstances of our engagement, but I assure you my heart is in the right place."

Her father looked at Tyler's outstretched hand for a moment before setting the gun aside and shaking it. "I appreciate your apology. As for your heart, we'll see how I feel about that at the end of the evening."

Tyler nodded and forced a smile, but his nerves now felt like they were in the middle of a hurricane. He didn't think the man would actually shoot him, especially on camera, but it was obvious he would have to earn his respect and the presence of the gun made that prospect a little more daunting.

∽

Laney shook her head as she joined Tyler on the couch. She had known her parents had reservations - she did too - but she had not expected her father to really have the gun out. He had often threatened to greet her boyfriends that way when she was in high school, but she had never found out if he was serious having never had a boyfriend in high school. And though she had dated in college and after college, those relationships had never lasted long enough to bring the men home to meet her family.

"Let's talk about this contract," her father said. He had put the gun beside him on the coffee table, but it still drew the attention in the room like a beacon. "I hear you got paid to propose to my daughter."

Tyler took a deep breath. "They gave me a contract when I came on the show before I even met Laney. That contract paid a sum of money as long as I completed the show. When I began falling for your daughter, I spoke with the producers about stepping down and voiding the contract, so I could pursue her. Their solution was to have her come on the show. When she fell, I knew she was the one for me and I again tried to exit the show, but their solution was the proposal. Yes, they did offer me more money and they did set a timeline for our wedding but at that point I knew I wanted to marry Laney anyway." He flashed her a warm smile. "So, the extra money was just frosting on the cake, so they say."

Her father sat back and rubbed his chin. "You would have married her anyway?"

"I would have left the show to pursue her and

eventually proposed yes. This may have sped up my timeline, but it did not create something out of nothing."

"And what exactly would Laney do on your ranch?"

"Dad!" Laney could not believe he was giving Tyler such a hard time. However, it was a good question. There wasn't much of a need for a makeup artist in his small town.

"She'll do whatever she wants. I'm not looking for someone to be an assistant on the ranch. I'm looking for a partner, so if she wants to assist then that's fine, but if she wants to do something else, that's okay too."

"And what if what I want to do means being away from you for months on end?" Laney hadn't meant to say the words out loud but even though she uttered them quietly, Tyler heard them and turned to her.

"We'll figure it out. If you want to keep doing makeup, we'll figure it out."

But Laney wondered if it would be that easy. Working for a studio would mean being gone through filming season at least. Plus, there would be the added cost of living somewhere while working. If she worked for a modeling agency like Madame Bonavich's, then it might be even worse. She'd need to be there full time or have the money to fly back and forth. Laney didn't know how much they had given Tyler, but she doubted it would stretch very far doing that.

"Tyler, maybe we rushed things. Maybe we need to talk about this more. I care about you, but if I keep doing makeup, I might never be there. You want a partner, but what kind of partner will I be if I'm never around?"

A heavy silence fell in the room as all eyes turned on Tyler. Out of the corner of her eye, Laney saw Maryanne shake her head, but she wasn't going to pretend everything was okay just for the cameras.

Tyler ran a hand through his dark hair. His shoulders rose and then fell with a sigh as if carrying an invisible weight on them. "I agree it's not an ideal situation, Laney, but I don't want to give up. God gave me peace about going on the show. He gave me peace about proposing to you. I don't believe He will forsake us now."

Laney wanted to believe that too, but she wasn't as sure. She'd seen her fair share of relationships destroyed because of distance. However, at the same time, she didn't have a permanent job as a makeup artist yet. In fact, she didn't have a permanent job at all. The studio had offered to keep her on for another month or so until the regular girl returned, but after that, she was on her own. Maybe, after that time, she could look for a job in Tyler's town. It could pay the bills until she found another makeup job, and if she was lucky, it would be something she enjoyed even more. "You're right," she said squeezing his hand. "God brought us this far together. We will just have to trust He carries us through."

23

Laney sighed as she stepped off the airplane. She was glad to be back with Tyler - the distance had been just as rough as she'd thought it would be - but the next few months worried her. Her job with the studio was over as they were taking a month-long hiatus and when they returned their regular girl would be back. Though they had sent her name out with references, none had called yet, so she was arriving in Fredericksburg with enough money for a month. Maybe two. Nancy had offered their spare bedroom for as long as Laney needed it, but she didn't want to start a friendship by imposing any longer than she had to.

Her heart lifted, however, when she spotted Tyler. Though they had face timed every evening to do their devotionals, it wasn't the same as seeing him in person. She waved and quickened her pace, jumping in his arms when she reached him.

"I've missed you," he said nuzzling her ear. His arms wrapped around her waist and he tugged her closer to him.

"Me too." She pushed back against him as desire coursed through her, "but we're in the airport."

"I don't care where we are or who sees us. It's been too long since I've kissed you." His lips moved from her ear to her lips and Laney gave in. She'd missed kissing him too.

"Get a room," a woman said as she passed them, and Laney pulled back in embarrassment. The kiss had turned from innocent to passionate too quickly. Perhaps it was a good thing their wedding was in three months.

Tyler chuckled and wrapped his arm around her waist. "Come on. Let's get you settled. Aaron and Nancy are waiting."

Laney followed him to the baggage claim area, and after securing her few bags - she had only brought what she took to California - she followed him to his truck.

"Do you realize," he asked as he opened the passenger seat for her, "that this is the first time we've been together without cameras since the day you were in the hospital?"

"I don't know about you, but I'm relieved. I'm a little tired of being on camera all the time." Even their last few meetings with the wedding planner had been filmed. "A little something to entice the audience and keep them interested," Justin had said, but Laney was tired of enticing the audience.

"I'm so relieved." He grinned at her as he started the truck, "but the cameras kept me from losing myself with you. I guess Nancy and Aaron will have to be that accountability now."

Laney felt a heat crawl up her cheeks at his innuendo. She too had felt that desire more than once to know him on a more intimate level, but they had both agreed to wait until marriage. "I just hope I won't be too much of a burden on Nancy and Aaron. I hate having to stay with them-"

He cut her off. "Nonsense. They adore you and are happy to be helping. Besides, I have no doubt you'll find a job soon."

Laney hoped so. She wasn't expecting to find a makeup job, but she would take anything for now.

TYLER GLANCED over at Laney as he drove. Though he put on a confident air, a tiny piece of him worried. What if Laney couldn't find a job in town? What if she hated what she could find? Would she want to leave and go back to the city?

He'd brought his concerns to God and he'd hashed them out with Aaron and Nancy, but that didn't make them any less real. Nor did it lessen them. However, he wasn't going to share them with Laney. He knew she was struggling with her own doubts, and though he wanted to be open and honest with her, he didn't think she needed his hesitations added to her own.

"Here we are," he said when he pulled up in front of

Nancy and Aaron's house. He was thankful his friends had opened their doors to Laney though not really surprised. Nancy and Aaron were like that, and they would do just about anything for Tyler. They had certainly been there for him when he decided to give up drinking and detox.

The front door opened as they exited the car, and Nancy, grinning from ear to ear, hurried out to them. "You're here! I'm so glad you're here."

Tyler chuckled at his friend's exuberance. He hoped it would ease Laney's fears of being a burden.

As Nancy enveloped Laney in a hug, Tyler retrieved her suitcases from the truck bed.

"Thank you for letting me stay," Laney said. "I promise I won't be here too long."

"Nonsense. I'm excited to have you here. It will be like having a sister and I've always wanted one." She flashed a wink in Tyler's direction as she led Laney into the house.

Tyler sent up a quick prayer thanking God for such wonderful friends.

"Mind if I join you?"

Laney looked up surprised to see Nancy in the kitchen. She thought they had gone to bed hours ago. Unable to sleep, she'd wandered in looking for some ice cream and a good place to read.

"Of course. It's your kitchen. I hope it's okay I had some ice cream. I can replace it tomorrow."

Nancy smiled and shook her head. "Mi casa es su casa, but you've hardly touched the ice cream. You want to talk about it?"

Laney stared down at her bowl. Her ice cream had melted into a murky liquid mottled with color. Laney imagined her feelings would look the same if they could be painted. "I'm worried about finding a job. I've never not had one and now I feel like I'm depending on you and Tyler…. it's a little depressing and nerve wracking."

Nancy placed a hand on her arm. "It's normal to feel like that, but it's also okay to accept help. God made us social creatures, so we would help each other. We were there for Tyler when he needed us, and we're here for you now."

Laney's eyes teared up at the kind words, and she dropped her gaze to her bowl. "I don't know what I did to deserve friends like you guys but thank you."

"You're welcome, and about that job… I may know of something. It probably won't pay what you're used to, but I've been looking for an assistant for my debate team. Tyler said you used to do competitions, right?"

Laney nodded. She had told Tyler all about her high school trips to compete in acting and debate, but she hadn't realized he'd told Nancy.

"Well," she smiled, "I happen to be the debate teacher at our local high school. We're probably smaller than your school was, but I've wanted to get the kids involved in tournaments. However, I've needed someone knowledgeable who could help coach the kids and go on trips with us."

A spark of interest blossomed in Laney's chest.

"You'd have to pass the background check, and you'd start as a para which, I'm not going to lie, the pay isn't great, but it's a job. It's something you were interested in, and if you enjoy it, you could look into getting your teaching certificate and take it over."

"Take it over? But isn't that your job?"

Nancy smiled and leaned across the table. "It is, but I'm pregnant, and it's taken us so long to have a baby that I want to take a few years off to enjoy being a mother."

"Oh my gosh. Congratulations, Nancy." Laney dropped her spoon and rushed around to hug her new friend.

"Thank you," Nancy said returning the hug. "So, you see, you'd be helping me out as well as yourself."

"I'll do it." Laney didn't have to think about it. She'd loved competing in high school, and she knew she would enjoy it just as much now. It might be a 'Brainy Laney' thing to do, but she was okay with that. Perhaps 'Brainy Laney' wasn't so bad after all. She smiled as she thought about how in control God was. A few months ago, she'd been lonely, working a terrible job, and dreaming of a man who she'd barely even talked to. Now, she was surrounded by friends, about to do something she loved, and engaged to a wonderful man.

24

*L*aney sighed as she walked to her car. It had been another long evening prepping the students for a tournament tomorrow, but she finally felt they were ready. Now, she just had to make sure she was in bed before ten pm so that she would be able to function the next morning.

She pulled into the driveway of the small rental and turned off the car. It was a cheap Honda, but it was hers. Nancy had been kind enough to give her rides for the few weeks she lived with them, but finally Laney had saved enough to not only purchase the cheap Honda but to make the deposit on the rental house as well. The landlord, being a friend of Aarons, had even given her a month-to-month lease knowing that she would be moving in with Tyler after the wedding. Laney could hardly believe that was only a few weeks away.

She pulled out her keys to open the front door and dropped them in surprise when her cell phone began ringing. It was probably Tyler wanting to wish her goodnight since she had missed their nightly dinner. As she squatted down to grab her keys, she punched the button on her cell. "Hello?"

"Is this Laney Swann?"

Laney's fingers grasped the keys and she stood. This was not Tyler. "Yes, this is Laney Swann. Who is this?"

"My name is Madeline Perry, and I'm the head of Perry Modeling Agency. Peter gave me your name and a glowing recommendation. I'm looking for a makeup artist, and I'd like to interview you."

Laney's hand froze on the door knob. A modeling agency? This was the call she had been waiting months for, but her wedding was in a few weeks. Could she really start a new job now? Besides, she had a job. One that required her to be at the school at four in the morning. Still, this was her dream. Could she really turn it down?

"I would love that. I have to be somewhere tomorrow, but I could take a few days after that."

"That would be perfect. Give me your email address and I will have my assistant send you the flight information."

The woman was going to pay to fly her there for an interview? This was even better than she dreamed. "Fantastic." She rattled off her email address, thanked the woman, and then hung up the phone. Laney couldn't believe she had finally gotten an interview. She would have to tell Tyler, but it could wait until tomorrow. Tonight, she needed to grab some food, brush her teeth, and crawl into bed.

Tyler tried to keep his face emotionless as he listened to Laney tell him about the job interview. He knew this was what she had always wanted, but he had hoped she had found fulfillment working with the kids at the school. Perhaps it was selfish of him, but he didn't want her working in California. He wanted her here with him.

"What do you think?" Her eyes pleaded for him to be okay with it, and Tyler knew that's what he would do. He had told her father he wouldn't expect her to stay at the ranch if she didn't want to. Now, he was having to back up those words.

Tyler picked up her hand and rubbed his thumb across the back. He was so afraid, but he couldn't tell her that. He couldn't say that he didn't want her to go because he feared she might never come back. He couldn't say those words not because he didn't think she couldn't handle hearing them but because it wouldn't be fair to send her off with his fears. Tyler could see she had her own fears she was dealing with. There was no need to add his own.

"I think it's a great opportunity," he said slowly. Would this be the last time he got to hold her hand like this? He should relish the feeling just in case.

"And?"

"And I think you should go. Interview at least. I told you that I didn't want to hold you back, that we would make it work no matter what you wanted to do. If you get this job, it will make it a little harder, but nothing is impossible."

She scooted closer to him on the couch and placed her hand under his chin. He had kept his eyes down as he spoke, and she lifted his face now until they met her gaze. "Thank you, Tyler. I love you. I know you're scared, but I feel like I'll regret it if I don't go."

He nodded wanting to speak but not trusting his voice around the lump that had begun to form. He didn't want her to have any regrets. If they were going to marry - and he hoped they still would - he wanted to be sure it was what she wanted.

Her eyes remained on his, and he knew she was seeking reassurance. He cleared his throat. "Well, we should probably pray about this. Your safety and God's will to be done."

"That would be amazing."

He took both of her hands in his. They had done this nearly every day, but today felt different. "Lord, we thank you for this time together. We don't always understand Your will, but we seek to follow it. Help Laney to know if this is your will for her. Open doors if it is and close them if it's not. Grant her safe travels, and-" his voice caught. He was about to say, 'bring her back to me,' but this was Laney's prayer, not his. After she left, he could pray those words all he wanted, but right now he wanted this to be about her. However, he had no words for what to say next, so he ended lamely with, "amen."

When he opened his eyes, he could see hers glistening with unshed tears. He had made her happy and that felt good. He just hoped it wouldn't be the last time. The old saying, 'if you love someone, let them go,' fluttered through his mind. It was easier said than done, though, when all he wanted to do was pull her against his chest, wrap his arms around her, and feel her heart beat against his.

"I better go pack," she said and ran a finger under her eye. He saw the shine of wetness on it before she turned away and pushed herself up from the couch.

He followed suit to stand beside her. "Do you need a ride to the airport?" The thought of driving her there killed him, but at least it would mean more time.

She shook her head and fidgeted with the cross around her neck. "No, she's hired a car to pick me up. Royal treatment, I guess you could say."

He could think of another word. Bribery, bait, enticement, but none of those sounded as nice. "All right, well, call me when you get there so I know you landed okay. I guess I'll see you in a few days."

"Yeah."

He pulled her into his arms and placed his mouth against her neck. "I love you Laney."

"I love you too."

And then she was gone, and for the first time in

months, Tyler felt the monster awaken inside of him. It clawed about his stomach, seeking a handhold to use in order to crawl out. Tyler reached for his phone and punched in the number he knew from memory. "Aaron? I need you."

25

Laney stared in awe at the modeling agency. It wasn't quite as large as Madame Bonavich's had been, but it was close. Glass windows granted an expansive view of downtown and rich colors filled the office.

"Welcome, Laney, I'm Madeline Perry. I'm so glad you could make it."

The outstretched hand was slender which fit the woman in front of her. Though not short, Madeline was Twiggy-thin, and her severe blond haircut made her appear even thinner. Dark liner accentuated her grey eyes that looked like a storm. Calm now, but Laney wondered what they transformed into if Madeline were angry.

"Thank you. Me too."

"I heard you ended up becoming a contestant on Peter's show. I'm sorry I don't watch it, but some of my girls have auditioned for it before." As Madeline sauntered toward a massive desk, Laney wondered how her slacks stayed on. The woman appeared to have no hip bones to keep them up.

"I did, and I ended up with the Cowboy. Tyler."

"Oh, a cowboy. How quaint. I don't suppose you kiss and tell though." Her eyes raked over Laney as if appraising her. Laney felt her face flush. She didn't know if the woman were asking for details or hinting at something else. Neither thought made her comfortable.

"I don't, but the wedding is in a few weeks and the studio is filming it. If you are interested, you could tune in."

Madeline's playful banter disappeared, "Are you planning a long honeymoon?"

"I... I don't know. We haven't really discussed it. Planning the wedding has been hectic enough." Laney couldn't believe the honeymoon hadn't come up until now. Had she just assumed the wedding planner was handling it?

"The reason I ask," Madeline said with a tight smile, "is because I need someone reliable. This job requires a lot of hours, and I can't have someone who's going to be gone for an excessive amount of time."

"Oh, I'm sure it wouldn't be excessive. A week, maybe two."

"Two would be too long, but if you can keep it at a week, we can continue the interview."

Warning bells sounded in Laney's head. Madeline hadn't seemed like Madame Bonavich over the phone or when Laney had first entered the office, but she was glimpsing similar traits now. Still, this was her dream job. Wasn't it?

"I'm sure we could manage a week." Why had she said that? It was like she couldn't help herself.

"Very good. Then let me introduce you to Natalie."

"Natalie?"

"Yes, my lead makeup artist. You didn't think I was hiring you for lead, did you?"

Laney's mouth opened, but she had no words.

"Oh, you did." Madeline laughed. "I'm sorry, Laney, I'm looking for an assistant. No one hires a lead they haven't worked with. Not in this business. It doesn't matter how good your references are."

Laney knew then that she no longer wanted to be in this business. She enjoyed makeup, and she had thought it was what she wanted, but being here didn't hold the same appeal it once had. She missed her students and her friends. "No, I'm the one who's sorry. I've wasted your time though I didn't mean to. I'm afraid I've realized this isn't my life anymore. My life is back in Texas with my Cowboy."

Tyler raked his hand across his chin. "I thought I was

past this, you know? This urge to drink, but Laney leaving," he shook his head, "I guess it hit me hard."

"Don't be so hard on yourself," Aaron said as he sat across from Tyler. "It was sudden, but that doesn't mean she's going to take it. Nancy says she's a natural with the kids. People like that? They realize their true calling. It might take her a while, but I think she'll come around."

"And what if she doesn't? What if she ends up another Sierra or Dierdre or-"

"Stop. You can't keep beating that dead horse. Yes, you've had crappy luck with women, but you're not your dad."

"I never said I was."

"No, but you've been acting like it. It's like you've been trying so hard to prove you won't be like him that you're ending up doing the same thing. Only difference is you're pushing the women away before you marry them instead of after."

Tyler thought back over his relationships. Had he been pushing them away? Certainly not outright but subconsciously, maybe. Perhaps he wanted a family so badly that he had been putting pressure on the women he had dated unknowingly. "I had no idea," he said shaking his head.

"Look man, we all have something, but you can't let your fear and insecurity of losing Laney drive her away. Be supportive and I promise you that she'll be back."

"You're right. Thank you, Aaron. Once again you've saved my bacon."

Aaron clapped a hand on his shoulder. "That's what friends are for, man. You get the urge to drink again, you call me, okay? Any time, day or night."

Tyler nodded and shook Aaron's hand. "Thank you." He wasn't sure he wanted to leave yet. The demons were louder when he was alone and thinking about Laney, but he knew Aaron had things to do for Nancy. She was nearing month six of her pregnancy and not able to do everything she could before.

He pulled the front door open and stopped short. Was he imagining things or had Aaron actually wished her home? "Laney?"

"Hi, Tyler, I went by your ranch first, but when you weren't there, I figured you might be here."

An invisible vice squeezed his heart. If she was seeking him out this soon after her interview, was it to say goodbye for good? "How did the job interview go?"

She twisted her mouth into an endearing smirk. "Oh, it was good." His heart fell. "But it's not the job for me."

His eyes flew to hers. Had he heard her correctly? "You didn't take it?"

The corners of her mouth twitched before breaking into a wide grin. "Nope. I realized when I got there that I didn't want that life anymore. Everything I want is right here. With you."

He didn't have words, but he didn't need them. In two steps, he covered the distance between them and pulled her into his arms. His lips pressed against hers, fear and love and relief pouring out as he tugged her closer. Her hands wound around his neck and his slid down to her waist. Heat burned between them and though he didn't want to, Tyler forced himself to end the kiss before he compromised their promise.

"Everything I want is right here too," he whispered into her ear, and she laid her head on his chest.

26

Tyler looked around in awe as he and Laney stepped off the airplane. He'd never been to Hawaii and it was more beautiful than he'd even imagined. And hot. It felt a lot like Houston only a little less muggy, and he was still inside.

Bronwyn, their wedding planner, waved at them from across the room. He nudged Laney and pointed to the right. "Looks like our ride is here."

Beside him she sighed. "It's been nice having her handle the details I guess, but her personality-"

"Is grating?" he finished.

"To say the least," Laney said with a laugh.

Tyler wasn't sure if Bronwyn's personality was true or an act for whatever unknown reason, but she was the epitome of a valley girl. Her use of the word 'like' was extraordinary and exhaustive.

"Oh my gosh. Isn't this like so amazing?" she asked

when they neared her. She held two leis in her hands which she placed around their necks. "You totally can't land in Hawaii without being leid." Then she laughed, and it was a grating high-pitched sound that reminded Tyler of nails on chalkboards. Laney squeezed his hand in a death grip.

"We're a little beat from the plane ride, Bronwyn. Maybe we can go check into the hotel now?"

Her laugh faded, and her eyes widened. "Of course, silly me. I'm so sorry. You must be exhausted. Follow me."

She led the way down to the baggage claim and then out to where a limo was waiting.

"I have kind of missed this treatment," Tyler said with a small smile as he and Laney climbed into the back. "Haven't you?"

"Not in the least," she said with an eye roll.

He pulled her to his side and wrapped his arm tightly around her. "How about now?"

"What are you doing?" she asked as she twisted to look up at him.

"The last time we were in a limo together, you hit your head on my chin falling for me. I don't want you to have a big goose egg before the ceremony."

Her eyes narrowed, and she jabbed a finger at his chest. "I fell because the driver slammed on the brakes. Nothing more."

"That's not how I remember it," he said with a sly grin.

"Ah, you guys are so cute."

Even Bronwyn's voice couldn't break the moment between Tyler and Laney. Tomorrow she would be his wife, and Tyler couldn't think of anything he wanted more than to have her by his side forever.

He turned his attention out the window and took in the beautiful scenery. He loved Texas, but it sure didn't have the same tropical appeal that Hawaii did. The road led them close enough that he could see the ocean and beaches out the window, and it did not surprise him when the limo pulled up in front of a large hotel.

He *was surprised* by the paparazzi that greeted them as they stepped out of the limo.

"Tyler, Laney, do you really think you're in love? Do you believe a marriage that started on a reality show can last? Is it true they paid you to propose?"

Tyler sneaked a glance at Laney and was dismayed to see the tightness in her face. They had faced all these questions four months ago when he first proposed, and he thought they had gotten past them, but her body language suggested otherwise. He wondered if their unusual beginning would haunt them forever.

Grabbing Laney's hand tighter, he pulled her closer to him and forged through the reporters like a linebacker. The door to the hotel was just a few feet away, and he yanked it open with one swift motion. Blissful silence greeted them on the other side.

He whirled on Bronwyn. "Are reporters going to be at our wedding? Because if they are, we won't walk. We'll happily get married elsewhere without the fanfare."

Bronwyn's eyes were wide with surprise and perhaps a trace of hurt. "No. I planned no reporters, but they probably caught wind when our crews began arriving. I promise you that even though we are televising the wedding, it will be tasteful."

"Can we just get to our rooms?" Laney asked. Her voice was pinched yet emotionless.

"Of course. I'll have the driver bring your bags up after I get you checked in."

LANEY SIGHED as she fell back on the bed. The day had started off so good and then the reporters had been at the hotel. She had forgotten how pervasive the cameras were and though she wanted to marry Tyler, there was a part of her that wanted to call the wedding off, sneak off to some quiet chapel, and elope. Plus, they had drug up old questions and insecurities. Ones that she thought she had gotten over, but clearly, she hadn't. Strange how in high school she had just wanted people to notice her and now she just wished they would leave her alone.

She and Tyler had been lucky in Fredericksburg. People in town knew of their television romance but hadn't seemed to care and only a few rabid fans had bothered to find them there. Her students who watched the show had been the most excited ones, but even they had lost their celebrity fascination after a week. Laney wondered why people even still cared about her and Tyler's marriage.

A knock sounded at her door and she considered ignoring it, but it was probably her luggage and she needed to hang up her wedding dress. "Just a minute," she called when the knocking continued, but when she opened the door, it wasn't the bell hop she saw but Maryanne, Jennifer, Meredith, Tracey, and Steven - her closest friends from high school. "Oh my gosh, what are you doing here?"

Steven looked at the women. "I thought we were attending a wedding. Are we not attending a wedding?"

"No, I mean early. What are you doing here early?" She'd expected Maryanne early and Nancy as they would be her bridesmaids, but the others were an extremely nice surprise.

"I thought it might be fun if we had a reunion before your wedding," Maryanne said with a shrug, "since you aren't having a bachelorette party or a rehearsal dinner."

"You are the best. Get in here." The fears and worries from moments before faded away as her old friends filed into her room. Maryanne, Meredith, and Jennifer sat down on the bed while Tracey, Steven, and Laney pulled chairs from the breakfast table closer to the bed.

"Okay, I have to know what everyone has been up to," Laney said as she looked from face to face.

"Fine, but then we want to hear all about Tyler and this crazy romance," Jennifer said.

"Yeah, leave it to you to have the most amazing wedding story of all of us," Meredith said. "I mean I just married my college sweetheart."

"I married one of my coworkers," Jennifer said, "but it wasn't amazing like this unless you count our Star Wars wedding as exciting."

"You didn't," Laney said with a laugh.

"Yes, I did. Walked down the aisle as Princess Leia with buns and everything."

The group continued to share stories for the next few hours. Tracey and Steven had yet to marry, but Meredith had a daughter and Jennifer had dogs she considered her children. Meredith had gone into social work which didn't surprise Laney as she had experienced foster care for a short time in high school and developed a heart for kids like herself. Jennifer was a drama teacher. Also not surprising. She'd generally held the leads in school plays. Tracey and Steven had both gone into law but not together.

"So, are you really going to live in Texas after the wedding?" Jennifer asked. "I seem to remember you getting out of the state as fast as possible after high school."

Laney chuckled. "Yeah, I think I was running from myself after high school. I wanted to get away from the people who had never noticed me and start over, but somewhere in there I lost who I was for a few years. Tyler helped me find that girl again, and believe it or not, I'm working at a high school, coaching kids for UIL tournaments."

"Oh, I can believe it," Steven said. "I always figured you'd become a teacher."

"Because I was 'Brainy Laney?'"

"No, because you loved it. You loved school and learning. You came to school even when you felt awful because you were afraid you might miss something."

He was right, and as Laney thought back, she realized in running from her nickname, she had run from the best part of her - the part that loved learning and found joy in a good book. How far would she have changed herself in seeking to be noticed had she not gone on the show and met Tyler? She shuddered at the thought and suddenly all the stupid insecurities she had been focused on when she first entered the hotel became just that. Stupid insecurities. She didn't care that she and Tyler had met in a nontraditional way or that he had gotten paid when he proposed to her. What she cared about was that he had helped her find herself again, and she couldn't wait to spend the rest of her life with him.

27

Laney enjoyed the perks that came with a celebrity wedding. Though she'd had to get up early, the massage, facial, and mani pedi had been worth the lack of sleep. Now she sat in a chair letting an amazing hairdresser twist her blond hair into a fabulous style as another makeup artist perfected her face. Maryanne and Nancy were enjoying a similar treatment just a few feet away.

"It is beautiful," the hairdresser said stepped back and Laney had to agree. Her blond locks fell in perfect waves against her shoulders.

The makeup artist finished applying her lipstick and then Laney slipped out of her street clothes and into her dress. It too was something she never could have afforded - a strapless Vera Wang that hugged her curves in all the right ways. Red, pink, and white roses made up her bouquet, and the beautiful silver locket the studio had given her that hung around her neck completed her image. They had even supplied it with a picture of Tyler.

Maryanne and Nancy each had their dresses paid for as well and they had even tailored Nancy's for free to accommodate her growing belly. The soft pink of their dresses matched the color of her roses perfectly.

"Are we ready to get married?" Bronwyn asked.

Laney had to admit as they walked to the venue that Bronwyn had done a fabulous job. Not only was the dress perfect, but Bronwyn had set up wooden fences around a section of the beach where the ceremony would take place. It was like they had transported Tyler's ranch to the beaches of Hawaii, and it was perfect.

White chairs filled the beach and delicate bows of tulle hung across the backs of them and down the aisle. They had strewn red, pink, and white flower petals across the white carpet runner than covered the beach and a grand gazebo stood at the far end. Laney could just make out Tyler looking handsome in his tux next to Aaron and another friend.

"You look amazing," Laney's father said as he held out his arm. It had taken a few months but eventually her father had warmed to Tyler and given them both his blessing.

"Thanks Dad."

Laney watched as Nancy and then Maryanne made their way down the aisle. She barely registered the cameras filming the ceremony. Bronwyn had been right. They were tasteful, and no reporters were in sight.

When the music shifted, she made her way up the aisle with her father. Though she wouldn't have placed them there, it did not surprise Laney to see Peter, Justin, and the women from the show who had been promised a slot in the Maui spinoff sitting in the second row. At least they were all smiles today.

As she walked past them, Tyler consumed her focus. She had almost given up on getting married and would never have imagined marrying someone she had known less than a year, but here she was. And she knew it was right.

The pastor began to speak as she handed off her bouquet and took Tyler's hands, but her brain refused to focus on his words. Instead she focused on Tyler's beautiful sapphire eyes, the ones she would get to look into every day, and his dashing smile that she would get to wake up to every morning. She wouldn't have thought it possible, but all the angst and all the worry was worth it for this moment - when she would get to call him her husband.

TYLER'S HEART thudded as he slid the ring on Laney's finger. He was so focused on how beautiful she was that he barely heard the pastor ask for the rings. Thankfully Aaron was paying more attention and tapped his elbow. "With this ring, I thee wed." The words sounded simple, but Tyler felt the weight of them. He was bound to Laney now, but then again, he'd been bound to her since the first day when she fell into his arms.

She slipped his ring on his finger and repeated the words. He knew his smile must match her own because he felt like sunlight shone from every pore of his body.

"By the power vested to me by God and the state of Hawaii, I now pronounce you husband and wife. You may kiss your bride."

No words had ever sounded sweeter to Tyler, and he took no time leaning in and claiming Laney's lips as his own. Vaguely, he registered cheers and clapping, but he didn't care about them. He didn't care about the cameras or the contract. He simply cared about this moment. This moment that declared Laney was his wife.

When the kiss ended, he held up their hands. Another round of clapping erupted and then Tyler led the way down the aisle. He wasn't an aficionado of weddings, but he thought Bronwyn had done a fabulous job with the ceremony. As he followed her to another large roped off area, he realized she had done just as much work with the reception.

Beautifully decorated tables filled the area, and an elaborate floral arrangement sat in the center of each one. An outdoor DJ was set up to one side with large speakers mounted on tripods, and an open area sat in the middle which Tyler assumed was for dancing.

Bronwyn led them to the largest table, and the wedding party joined them shortly after. The rest of the guests filled in the tables. Waiters and waitresses in crisp white shirts and black pants appeared carrying trays of delicious foods. An appetizer, a salad, and an entree graced Tyler's plate, but while the food was divine, he couldn't focus on it. The thought of holding Laney in his arms and later in his bed consumed his mind.

Aaron gave a toast that he barely registered, but he flashed a smile whenever Aaron looked his way. Maryanne must have shared some funny moments from the show because the crowd chuckled, but he heard little of it as well.

The one thing he did hear was the call for the first dance. Actually, he wasn't sure he heard it so much as felt it when all the eyes in the area turned to him and Laney grabbed his hand.

She smelled sweet and flowery as he wrapped his arms around her, and he couldn't help stealing another kiss from her lips. "Thank you for being such a klutz," he whispered in her ear.

Her response was a silver bell of laughter and a punch in the arm. "Thank you for catching me. If you hadn't, I probably would have broken something and not been a part of the show at all."

"That would have been a travesty," he said.

"I couldn't agree more." Her arms tightened around his neck and Tyler enjoyed the feel of her in his arms.

The first dance ended, and Tyler reluctantly let go of her, so she could dance with her father and he with his mother. Before he knew it, the sun had drifted toward the horizon, the bouquet and garter had been tossed, and guests were beginning to issue their congratulations before disappearing up the beach.

"Well, you did it guys." It surprised Tyler to see Justin looking just as plastic but a little less smarmy standing before them. "I have to admit I wasn't sure you would make it, but you proved me wrong. Of course, before you ride off in the sunset, I need one more thing from you."

"What's that?" Laney asked beside him.

"We need a short interview with the two of you for the end of the episode."

"Fine, let's do it now." Tyler wasn't really in the mood to give an interview, but he wanted nothing to interrupt his night with Laney, so it made more sense to get it over with and off his mind.

Justin led them to where two chairs were placed together like a couch. The lights were already focused on it and a crew member Tyler didn't remember manned the camera. He and Laney sat down and then waited for smarmy game show host Justin to appear.

"In three, two, one." And there he was.

"Welcome ladies and gentlemen and thanks for tuning in with us tonight. I hope you enjoyed seeing Tyler's and Laney's wedding as much as I did. On the last episode, I told you I would catch up with them for a small question-

and-answer session, and I have. So, let's welcome Tyler and Laney Hall."

The camera panned their direction and Tyler tensed. He had not missed being on camera and he would not miss it after tonight.

"So, Laney, the viewers want to know if it was worth it going on the show and if you would do it again?"

Laney's body was stiff beside him, but her voice was warm and poised when she spoke. "Well, Justin, I didn't originally audition for the show, but I'll answer as best as I can. As for it being worth it," she smiled at Tyler, "I can definitely say yes. Would I do it again? That's a harder question. I would do it again if I knew going in what the final outcome would be, but it's a lot harder than people think."

"What made it so hard?" Justin pressed.

"At first it was watching Tyler with the other women and thinking I didn't have a chance, but it might have been even harder once I became a contestant because I had to deal with the women not liking me and yet being unable to get away from the situation. All those women in one house," she shook her head, "is stressful."

"It can be, but you handled it well, and people want to know your secret. How did you guys find lasting love once the cameras stopped rolling?"

Laney gazed up at him. "We trusted God."

"And our hearts," Tyler added.

"And we let ourselves fall," Laney said with a wide smile.

Tyler matched her grin and squeezed her hand.

"One more thing, Laney. I know you were filling in for us and when the show ended, you were looking to continue your work as a makeup artist. I wanted to be the first to let you know that Elite Modeling Agency reached out to us and wanted to offer you a position on their team. What do you say?"

Laney took a deep breath and stared evenly at Justin. "I would say thank you for the offer, but that isn't my life now. My life is with my husband on his ranch." She squeezed Tyler's hand and smiled at him.

"Well, there you have it folks. Thanks for joining us tonight and thank you Laney and Tyler for letting us share this day with you. We wish you all the best and we'll see you at home next time on 'Who Wants to Marry a Cowboy.'"

The camera stopped rolling and the lights turned off leaving Tyler and Laney staring at each other under the stars.

"You handled that well. You're kind of a natural on camera."

She chuckled and laid her head on his shoulder. "I think I'm done with cameras for a while. I'm perfectly content to just be Mrs. Hall. Well, almost perfectly content."

"Almost? What are you missing?"

She looked up at him with twinkling eyes and a mischievous grin. "A baby."

His heart soared as he leaned down and kissed her

again. "That I can certainly help with," he whispered in her ears.

"I thought maybe you could," she said as she kissed him again.

As the sun set around them, Tyler couldn't help but smile at the way things had turned out.

The End!

AUTHOR'S NOTE

FIRST OFF, let me say how glad I am that you read this book. When my friend Evangeline Kelly and I brainstormed this bride idea, I had no idea what I was going to write. Then I wrote The Billionaire's Cowboy Groom and my readers told me they wanted more cowboys. I thought 'I'm from Texas, I can do cowboys.' But the truth is, there weren't really many true cowboys in Lubbock, Texas where I grew up. So, I still had to do some research.

This book was originally titled The Cowboy's Unlikely Bride because I was going to make it an opposites attract book, but I just couldn't make the idea gel in my head. I liked Laney and I liked Tyler but in order to make them unlikely, I would have to change one of them, and I just couldn't do it. So I changed the title of the book instead.

I've never been on a reality dating show, but I was on Wheel of Fortune once and yes, they did airbrush us. It was Teacher's Week 2008 or 2009 I think, but good luck finding the episode. I don't think it exists anywhere but my Tivo anymore. And yes, I still have the Tivo just because my Wheel of Fortune episode is on it. And because I know you're thinking it, I wasn't the big winner, but I almost won a trip to Hawaii. Gently Lapping Waves was the puzzle that would have sent me there, but with only two letters remaining, my brain froze and I picked the wrong letter. One day, I will make it to Hawaii.

Anyway, I thought it would be fun to bring the reality show into it. I don't always watch The Bachelor, but I've seen a few seasons (shh, don't tell anyone. Trista and Ryan were my favorite) but I was surprised to find out the women had to do their own makeup and they didn't get paid.

And making Laney a makeup artist seemed to work with her personality of trying to be someone else. Laney is actually a lot of me. In fact, I went by Laney for a time in high school. I was a debater and participated in UIL tournaments. Thank you Ms. Patridge for taking us. I really did have a core group of friends named MaryAnne, Jennifer, Meredith, Tracey, and Steven, so this book more than any other is a part of me. The same could be said for the special epilogue that you can get for free because you purchased this book.

If you loved this book and want to follow Laney and Tyler a little longer, simply email a copy of your receipt to realitybridebonus@gmail.com and I will send you the epilogue which turned into more of a short story in and of itself for free. It's my way of saying thank you for taking a chance on me and my books.

And if you've enjoyed reading this author's note so far (and really, how could you not?) I am offering, for today only, a page where you can sign up for my weekly newsletter for the low, low price of absolutely nothing.

Included in this weekly newsletter is many wonderful things like pictures of my adorable children, chances to win awesome prizes, new releases and sales I might be holding, great books from other authors, and anything else that strikes my fancy and that I think you would enjoy.

Even better, I solemnly swear to only send out one newsletter a week (usually on Tuesday unless life gets in the way which with three kids it usually does). I will not spam you, sell your email address to solicitors or anyone else, or any of those other terrible things.

Join me here and receive a free novella as my thank-you gift for choosing to hang out with me. It's fun and entertaining. I promise.

Prayers and blessings,
Lorana

29

NOT READY TO SAY GOODBYE YET?

∽

THE COWBOY'S Reality Bride is the first book in the multi-author Blushing Bride series. While each book written by a different author in the series will be a stand alone, I have decided to make mine a series. If you are reading on Amazon, the numbers may look confusing, but just know that my books will twine together.

With that in mind, the next book in the Blushing Bride series will be The Producer's Unlikely Bride (yep, I figured out ho to make that opposites attract thing work, but only because Justin was dislikable in this book).

The book opens after the Maui season ends and we see Justin at his worst. Don't give the guy too hard of a time yet. He's had a past, but when his future pairs him with a romance author who always sees the glass half full, it might be too much for him.

The Producer's Unlikely Bride

A reality dating show host who no longer believes in love.

Justin Miller is tired of hosting Who Wants to Marry a Cowboy. No, what he's tired of is seeing other people find love especially with his past. He wants nothing to do with romance and can't believe his luck when he gets stuck with a romance writer in a cottage at the beach.

She thrives on romance. If only she could find her own.

Ava McDermott believes in love. She should as she writes romance novels for a living, but she can't seem to find her own happily ever after. And she certainly isn't going to find it with the plastic Ken doll host she's stuck with. The time at the cottage was supposed to be relaxing and allow her to write.

The double edged bargain....

These two have only one thing in common. The ability to help one another, but can they keep to the rules or will their fake relationship turn into something more?

Read on for a taste of The Producer's Unlikely Bride....

30

THE PRODUCER'S UNLIKELY BRIDE PREVIEW

*J*ustin ran his fingers through his platinum blond hair. Every hair had a place, and it was integral that all of his lay in their right place. He wasn't looking for love - that ship had sailed a long time ago - but he was looking for a new job and the way to do that was to look perfect on this one. A reality show host had to ooze perfection and charm. Things Justin had in in spades which was why he'd had the job for a decade.

And 'Who Wants to Marry a Cowboy' paid well, but dealing with all the happy couples… Yes, that was the issue. It hadn't been so bad when only one of the couples lasted, but watching Tyler and Laney buck the system and find love even when it seemed impossible had reminded him of his own failed… No, he would not walk down that road again. The past need to stay there. Firmly locked behind a metal door with a dozen deadbolts.

He regarded the mirror one more time, and when he

was satisfied that he looked as good as he could, Justin sprayed a liberal coating of hair spray across his hair. It was the last show of the Maui edition, and the salty ocean breeze always ruffled his hair. Tonight, he wanted it to stay in place. One more spray wouldn't hurt. Just for good measure. When he had given his hair another coat, he placed the can down on the dresser, winked at his reflection, and then headed for the door.

Carl, the current Cowboy bachelor, would be waiting nervously at his bungalow as he had been every night. Justin wished they had never chosen him. Calling him indecisive was putting it mildly. Every time there was a ceremony, the man practically broke out in hives and spent half an hour waffling over one girl or the other with Justin who had to pretend to care. It didn't really matter who Carl picked. Once reality hit and they left the show, most couples didn't make it longer than six months. Tyler and Laney were the exception - not the rule.

He knocked on Carl's bungalow, unphased when the door opened and Carl, a sweaty, blotchy mess, greeted him by pulling him into the room. He clung to Justin's hand as if it were a life vest in the ocean. Cold, clammy wetness seeped into Justin's palm, and he bit his lip to keep from yelling at the man.

"Justin, I'm so glad you're here. I don't know if I can go through with this. Cara and Destiny are both great. I think I love them both. How am I supposed to choose?"

With as much tact as he could muster, Justin eased his hand from Carl's grip. The desperate need to run it down his pants to wipe off the sheen filled him, but he would not do it. He could feign empathy for a little longer. "You'll do it the way you've done it the whole show, Carl. You'll go with your gut. Choose the one you have the best connection with."

"But what if I'm wrong? What if I choose the wrong woman? I mean this is marriage we're talking about." Carl ran his hand across his chin as he paced the floor.

Justin tried not to roll his eyes. It was the same story over and over again. Every bachelor except Tyler and Kurt, the other one who had married his contestant, had said almost the exact same thing. They all believed they were making a choice that would affect their life but really only affected their next four to six months. Normally, Justin would say nothing, but today he couldn't keep his mouth shut. "No one lasts on this show, man. It doesn't matter who you choose."

Carl's mouth opened and closed then opened again. He look like a fish trying to get off a hook. His pacing stopped for a moment as his hand ran through his hair. "Are you saying this won't last? No matter what?"

Justin shrugged. He shouldn't have said that. Peter would eat him alive if he found out. But he was tired, he wanted to sleep, and the truth was that nearly no one did. "People have, but not many."

Carl crossed the room to stand in front of Justin. His eyes gleamed with a desperate intensity. "What did they have? What made them different?"

That was the million dollar question now wasn't it? If

Justin knew what kept them together, he could help Peter find similar couples in the future. If matches made on the show actually stayed together, it might skyrocket their viewing. Although Justin wasn't sure whether that was a good thing or not. On one hand, it might get him the exposure he wanted and a hosting role on a more popular show, but on the other, if the show grew too popular, he might not be able to leave.

None of that mattered to Carl who still stared at him with those dopey, hopeful eyes like the puppy who waits at the door for you to come home, but he had no words of wisdom for the cowboy. Didn't he know divorce rates were nearly sixty percent? It didn't matter if you met on a reality dating show or church, the numbers were almost the same.

Church. Huh. Justin hadn't realized it at the time, but thinking back now, he was almost certain the other couple who had lasted possessed a similar belief in God to Tyler and Laney. Surely that was coincidental though. His parents had been regular church attenders and they had still divorced. In fact, his father was on his third or fourth wife by now.

Justin shook his head to clear the wandering thoughts. He clapped a hand on Carl's arm and flashed his pep-talk smile. "They trusted their heart and didn't let fame go to their heads."

"Fame… . right." Carl nodded as he spoke, but Justin knew he was more focused on the fame than the letting it go to his head part. Carl was certainly no Tyler. It was obvious from the first meeting that he was on the show to get noticed.

He'd shown up with an extra tall hat and a thick southern drawl that wavered in its consistency - thicker when the women were around and barely noticeable when it was just the two of them. In addition, he had a wink for every woman in the room. He'd locked lips with at least three of them the first night, and unlike Tyler, he had made use of the overnight dates. For a man who seemed so worried now, he had certainly appeared flippant throughout the process.

"It's time. You ready?"

CLICK HERE to continue reading The Producer's Unlikely Bride

31

A FREE STORY FOR YOU

ENJOYED The Cowboy's Reality Bride? Not ready to quit reading yet? If you sign up for my newsletter, you will receive Once Upon a Star, the love story of Blake and Audrey, two of my Star Lake characters, right away as my thank you gift for choosing to hang out with me.

Once Upon a Star

A high school crush….

Blake was a nerd in high school. Never noticed. Looked over. So, it was no wonder that Audrey paid no attention to him, but now that she's back in town…

Audrey left Star Lake to pursue acting, but when she ends up pregnant and alone, she finds herself forced to return home.

Can Blake show Audrey a new side? Will she trust him enough to stay?

Read on for a taste of Once Upon a Star….

32

ONCE UPON A STAR PREVIEW

Audrey tried to peek around the nurses leaning over the silver table, obscuring the view of the thing she wanted to see most.

"Are you ready, Mom?" The head nurse, a kind, older woman with just a touch of gray in her dark hair, turned to Audrey, a tiny blue package in her arms.

Mom. The word had never applied to her, and she wasn't sure it fit. Was she ready? Probably not. Would she ever be completely ready? Probably not. But that didn't change reality. She tucked a strand of blond hair behind her ear and nodded.

"Here's your son." The nurse held the swaddled bundle out to her. Audrey opened her hands, unsure of what the nurse wanted her to do. The nurse's face softened and her warm brown eyes sparkled. With one hand, she adjusted Audrey's arms to place the tiny bundle in them. "Hold him like this." She demonstrated the proper technique. "You always want to support his head."

Audrey nodded, trying to keep her arms from shaking. She was afraid to breathe, afraid to move, but mostly afraid she'd drop the infant, so she kept her eyes glued to him. Would he shatter like a piece of glass? The image sent a shiver down her spine. She didn't want to find out.

The nurse's eyes twinkled as she watched Audrey adjust and readjust her holding position. "There is a bassinet here." She pointed at a clear plastic tub that looked like a large shoe box on top of a wheeled table. It didn't look comfortable to Audrey, and she wondered how a baby slept in it. "If you want to take him walking, you need to put him in the bassinet, okay?"

"Do I hold him the rest of the time?" As much as she was enjoying the baby in her arms, what happened when she needed to sleep or use the bathroom?

The woman chuckled. "You hold him as much as you want and put him down when you need a break. We'll come in every few hours to check on you, and we'll show you how to change his diaper and dress him. You'll be a pro before you know it. Don't worry." She patted Audrey's arm like her grandmother used to when she asked a silly question, and then the nurse walked out of the room, still smiling and shaking her head.

Audrey's eyes dropped to the sleeping baby. His shock of dark hair reminded her of his father, the olive-skinned Italian who had charmed her with his fast tongue. She hoped it was the only trait Cayden would get from him.

The world didn't need another heartbreaker. "I have no idea what we'll do, Cayden, but we'll figure something out."

Blake turned the glass on the countertop and glanced up at Max who leaned against the back counter, arms folded across his chest as if he were waiting for the answer to a question. The green of his plaid shirt matched the faded ball cap turned backwards on his head. "Sorry, did you say something? I'm distracted; it's just getting close to Christmas, and I miss Connie." A vision of the day she left popped into his head.

Blake opened the door, expecting to see Connie on the other side in her Sunday best. The church service started in half an hour. Though Connie stood there, his smile faded as he took in her jeans and t-shirt. There was no requirement of the patrons to dress up, but Connie always wore a dress or skirt. "What's going on?" Blake asked.

Connie bit her lip and her eyes fell to the ground. "I wanted to say goodbye."

"Goodbye?"

"I can't stay any longer, Blake." Her eyes lifted to meet his, and he saw the shimmer of liquid in them. "I hoped I could make a life here, but I'm a city girl. I miss the lights and night life. I miss the excitement."

"But, we were discussing marriage last week." Blake struggled to make her words compute in his brain.

"I know," she nodded, "and that's what got me thinking. The

thought of living the rest of my life here is depressing, so though I love you, I have to say goodbye." She leaned in and pecked his cheek before flashing a sad smile and walking back to her car.

With a heavy heart, Blake watched her drive away before shutting the door and leaning against it. His brain tried to make sense of her departure.

"I GET IT," Max said, leaning forward and dispersing Blake's memory. "It's not the same, but you're welcome to spend Christmas with Layla and me.

Blake offered a half smile. "I'll consider it, but it's your first Christmas together. You've been in love with that woman since I've known you and I don't want to be a third wheel. Besides, I'll probably hit the Christmas Eve service at church and spend the day with my mom. She's been lonely without my father around."

Max shrugged and turned back to the kitchen to finish serving the lunch crowd.

Blake took a bite of his hamburger, but while he knew it was delicious—Max was known for his burgers—it held no taste in his current mood. He fished a few dollars out of his wallet, laid the money on the counter, picked up his coat, and walked out the door.

The McAllister development where he worked sat a mile up the road, but as he still had fifteen minutes remaining on his lunch break, he decided to walk through downtown. His own house resided on the quiet outskirts of town, so other than hanging out with Max at The Diner, he didn't spend much time in the downtown area.

Blake pulled his coat tighter as the winter air bit through the heavy wool. Star Lake generally received one or two good snowfalls every winter, and though Christmas was still a few weeks away, the chill in the air made him believe the first snow was coming.

He didn't mind the snow, but he enjoyed it more when he had someone to share the experience with. Curling in front of the fireplace alone held little appeal.

AUDREY SHOVED the last item in her suitcase and pushed down on the bulging bag as she tugged on the zipper.

"Where are you going to go?" Desiree asked, leaning against the doorframe.

Desiree was Audrey's roommate, and the two were about as different as night and day. Where Audrey was pale and blond, Desiree had darker skin and long dark hair.

"The only place I can," Audrey said with a sigh. "Home."

The thought held little appeal. Her wealthy parents had given her access to her trust fund at eighteen, and Audrey had opted to move to LA to try her hand at acting. At first, it had been fun. She'd found a few jobs and been in a few commercials, but then the jobs had become fewer and farther between, and after she ended up pregnant, they had dried up completely. Now all the money she had saved was almost gone.

Desiree's nose scrunched in disgust. "You'd go back to that tiny town, why?"

"I haven't had a job in months Dez, my savings have run out, and I can't go to work without someone to watch Cayden. If I go home, I can get help from my parents until I get back on my feet."

At least she hoped they would help. They hadn't been too happy when she decided not to go to college, but she didn't think they would turn their grandson away, even if they didn't want to help her.

Desiree shrugged and flicked her hair behind her bony shoulder. "Nothing in the world would make me return to my crappy hometown."

Audrey knew Desiree's home life had been rough, but while she hadn't wanted to grow up under her mother's thumb, it hadn't been a bad childhood. "I don't know if I'll ever be back, but I wish you luck."

After a quick hug, Audrey picked up Cayden's car seat, slung her bag over her shoulder, and left the apartment she had called home for the last few years.

Click here to sign up for my newsletter and continue reading Once Upon a Star.

THE STORY DOESN'T END!

You've met a few people and fallen in love….

I bet you're wondering how you can meet everyone else.

Star Lake Series:
When Love Returns
Once Upon a Star
Love Conquers All
Heartbeats Series:
Where It All Began
The Power of Prayer
When Hearts Collide
A Past Forgiven
Sweet Billionaires Series:
The Billionaire's Secret
Brush with a Billionaire
The Billionaire's Christmas Miracle

The Billionaire's Cowboy Groom
The Lawkeepers series:
Lawfully Matched
Lawfully Justified
The Scarlet Wedding
Lawfully Redeemed
Lawfully Pursued
Voice of God:
The Still Small Voice
A Spark in Darkness
Stand Alones
Love Renewed
Blushing Brides Series:
The Cowboy's Reality Bride
The Reality Bride's Baby
The Producer's Unlikely Bride
The Cop's Fiery Bride
The Soldier's Stalwart Bride
Texas Tornado Series
Run With My Heart
Love on the Line
Touchdown on Love

Her children's early reader chapter book series:
The Wishing Stone #1: Dangerous Dinosaur
The Wishing Stone #2: Dragon Dilemma
The Wishing Stone #3: Mesmerizing Mermaids
The Wishing Stone #4: Pyramid Puzzles
The Wishing Stone Inspirations #1: Mary's Miracle

To see a list of all her books

> authorloranahoopes.com
> loranahoopes@gmail.com

DISCUSSION QUESTIONS

1. What was your favorite scene in the book? What made it your favorite?

2. Did you have a favorite line in the book? What do you think made it so memorable?

3. Who was your favorite character in the book and why?

4. Laney tried to change herself to be what she thought people wanted. What have you done to try and meet others' expectations instead of being yourself?

5. What do you think would be the hardest part about being on a reality dating show?

6. What did you learn about God from reading this book?

7. How can you use that knowledge in your life from now on?

8. What can you take away from Laney and Tyler's relationship?

9. What do you think would make the story even better?

ABOUT THE AUTHOR

Lorana Hoopes is an inspirational author originally from Texas but now living in the PNW with her husband and three children. When not writing, she can be seen kickboxing at the gym, singing, or acting on stage. One day, she hopes to retire from teaching and write full time.

CPSIA information can be obtained
at www.ICGtesting.com
Printed in the USA
BVHW082243070519
547697BV00001B/29/P